"If men could be contented to be what they are,
there were no fear in marriage."

—WILLIAM SHAKESPEARE, *All's Well That Ends Well*

HOOKED

a novel by john franc

 TIN HOUSE BOOKS / Portland, Oregon & New York, New York

Copyright © 2011 John Franc

Published by Tin House Books, Portland, Oregon,
and New York, New York
Distributed to the trade by Publishers Group West, 1700 Fourth St., Berkeley, CA 94710, www.pgw.com

Library of Congress Cataloging-in-Publication Data

Franc, John.
 Hooked : a novel / by John Franc. -- 1st U.S. ed.
    p. cm.
 ISBN 978-1-935639-15-2 (hardcover edition) -- ISBN 978-1-935639-16-9
(pbk. edition)
 1. Brothels--Fiction. 2. Sex addiction--Fiction. 3. Male friendship--Fiction. I. Title.
 PR6106.R38H66 2011
 823'.92--dc22

                              2011019921

First U.S. edition 2011
Printed in Canada
Design by Janet Parker
www.tinhouse.com

HOOKED

Oh boy, where to start. We were all long-married men with families in a city that we'd recently learned housed ninety-eight brothels, and of course it changed our lives. We were a captain of the merger industry, a medical professional, a biochemist, an accountant, a lawyer, a financier, an internet advertising wizard, a political advisor, a redistributor. We were every kind of man and apparently we were all monsters. We loved our wives, hated our wives, doted on our wives, ignored them, treasured them, pleasured them, and ultimately betrayed and defiled them. We had sons, daughters, house pets, favorite charities, long-term interests, avocations, home improvement projects, abstinences, and addictions. We loved each other, hated each other, cheated each other, belittled each other, questioned each other, taunted each other, and of course by absolute necessity trusted each other. One May evening we were sitting in one of our favorite haunts, a large rectangular room with a large rectangular bar bordered by shiny red leather bar stools, the walls lined with red-cushioned banks. We huddled close as the women approached in groups of threes and fours, most of them in their twenties but some in their thirties and a particularly dangerously alluring one clearly in her forties with the telltale crinkling of her skin. They had ten minutes to persuade us and some of them touched and felt us and some of them made us touch and feel them, and some of them did both, prodding their butts between our legs and working to find our apparent purpose. Everyone knows that there are several kinds of men, and we all knew which kind we were. Is there no way to begin in a neutral light?

Imagine a June birthday celebration at a park-side restaurant, six or eight families, the mothers situated at one table with bottles of wine and napkins on their laps, talking pleasantly, perhaps sometimes even excitedly, their hands for once free of sippy cups and plastic spoons and chocolate-coated grasping clutching fingers, while at a table across the terrace, at a considerable remove, the husbands lunched with the children, their ages three, four, five, six, eight, ten, eleven, twelve, thirteen, fourteen, and sixteen. Imagine that not only had the fathers agreed to this, but they'd asked for this—we'd asked for this—for the whole purpose and reward of fatherhood was to revel in it, to let it drown you.

Now imagine a night or an evening or an afternoon or even a morning two weeks earlier, and two or four or five of us slinking into a ground-floor apartment in a tony neighborhood of our gleaming city, and descending farther, below ground, into a warren of rooms and corridors, packed off first to one chamber for the parade of the available and then, once our choices had been made—you go first; no, after you, I insist; actually it is your turn to lead off and we need to be fair about this—separated into different rooms, each with a king bed and steps leading up to a whirlpool bath. How ever did this all start?

We met on the fields of our children's soccer league. We met at our children's birthday parties. We met at a gala dinner for women's rights. We met in church. Who can recall what our first words were—*hi, how are you, what is it that you do again, which child is yours, how long have you lived here, are you meeting a lot of people, which one is your wife, what is it that she does, would you like a drink, where do you live in the city, what kind of car do you drive, do you follow football, do you play much basketball, how far do you bike every day, do you have a favorite restaurant, do you want to meet for lunch sometime, let's do dinner, how about a game of poker*—but no one suspected where these words would lead us.

First, a brief survey.

In your opinion, which of the following forms of marital infidelity is most objectionable?

1. A solely physical tryst
2. A physical and emotional tryst
3. A paid-for tryst
4. All of the above
5. None of the above

Please return this response with your signed nondisclosure agreement. All results remain confidential.

We understand that we are male and you might not be. We recognize that we are ruthless and evil and immoral and indefensible, and you might not be. We admit that we are leading secret second lives and perhaps you are not, but certainly there are shades of you that you'd like no one to see. How—if ever—did you come to deny the existence of a divine creator? What is the worst thing you have ever done to another person? As a child, did you ever shoplift or cheat on a test or steal money from your father's wallet or your mother's purse or that envelope they kept in the kitchen pantry on the third shelf behind the ostensibly inexhaustible box of shredded wheat? Have you ever worn a new garment once and tried to return it to the shop? Have you knowingly accepted too much change from the cashier at the supermarket? Have you closed out a bill at a hotel without including items you have consumed from the minibar? Please conduct a quick inventory of all the pens, notepads, magazines, books, bath towels, and individual containers of soap, shampoo, hair conditioner, body lotion, and bath gel in your home. Are they all truly yours?

Of course we can't confide specifically who we are or where we live now because that would ruin everything, as if everything weren't already ruined.

No doubt you would prefer our story to take a more conventional form.

That spring we were playing poker at a bar perhaps not too far from where you live.

And who specifically are you?

Not all of us were there, but most of us were—A, B, C, D, E, F, G, H, and most important, I.

Our names cannot be released at this time due to personal or professional reasons or both. Most of our particular details have been altered or omitted to protect our true identities.

Why is it that our culture doesn't tolerate or accept what is tolerated and accepted by other cultures? Do you think perhaps that some or all of us were born in the wrong state or even the wrong country? Do Nevadans feel differently than the inhabitants of other states about the exposed peccadilloes of their politicians, movie stars, professional athletes, and numerous private citizens? Why is it that so many people not only rush to judgment but enjoy rushing to judgment? What are the most significant "values" that all of us share? Do you believe in the possibility of moral rehabilitation? What, in your opinion, is the correct morality of our time? How ironic is it that so many of the faces that populate our currency and so many of the names that grace our most substantial institutions are those of philanderers? Out of the following four philanderers, which is your favorite American president: _____, _____, _____, _____?

We'd dispensed with our first hand and were on our third or fourth pitcher of beer. With nine of us present, that seemed about right, don't you think? Most of us were nibbling at sandwiches. Most of us exercised regularly; none of us were smokers though some of us did smoke. Rarely. Okay, occasionally. Okay, frequently, but that wasn't what we told our life insurance providers.

"I can't believe you went alone."

"I had to. It had been at least nine days and I was curious about the place."

"Was it any good?"

"Fantastic. One of the best so far!"

"Oh, dude, we've got to go. How many were there?"

"Just three. But one was good and she was mine. We even cuddled afterward."

"GFE?"

"Pretty close to it."

We played quickly. Girlfriend Experience was our common goal.

"She said I looked so serious."

"They always say that about you."

"He *is* serious."

We were trying to get to all ninety-eight. One of us kept a list but no one would admit to tracking it too closely. We'd looked in on maybe fifteen and closed at maybe seven or eight, though frequently returning to the better places. Some of the others, it was true, were so vile and obviously unhygienic that we would never want to close there. We weren't that type of guy. Every place had the same sign on the wall, which we all respected. *The women here work of their own free volition and have the right to deny the client anything. In turn, depending on the circumstances, the client has the right to seek partial or full restitution.* Some of the places on our country's other coast were dinner clubs where the girls wore dresses with bows and picked you more than you picked them, and every tête-à-tête involved a careful mutual examination even prior to negotiation, and even then everyone's price was different. Those were complicated nights right out of a high school dance or a summer camp social.

"Why are you *so* serious, man?" we asked over the cards.

That was a good question, but it wasn't going to get answered.

The point is not to be shocking, but to be as truthful as we can be.

Perhaps you want to see us more clearly. Perhaps you don't want to see us at all.

The waiter, thank god, came with more beer. We all tried to meet for poker regularly—say, once every three weeks—but otherwise we were fragments of two and three and four and five guys who ricocheted around the city in taxis and on the metro and on foot, entering by night the more obviously exposed red light establishments and by day discovering the relatively discreet non-neon locales with their coy names: the

Sky Hotel, Between Sun and Sea, Duty Free, and, our favorite, the Pink Pearl. The rule was we tried never to go alone. The code was that should one of us ever be discovered, he would sink alone.

We can each remember our first time, whether it occurred years ago or months ago or sometime in between. A European city, an Asian island, a trailer outside of Vegas. A three-day "love you long time" bender, a thirty-minute escapade, a ten-second fiasco. The smell on our hands afterward, a lingering sentimentality, shock, the slow acceptance of the realization that it actually meant nothing to her, that we were forgotten as soon as we walked out the door, that it was the next customer's turn, and the next one after that, and the next one, and the next one. The gift of anonymity and the reward of unilateral gratification balanced by the fact that we gave up something physical and monetary and ultimately who could know what was ever given up in return? It was all slightly ambiguous and yet there was nothing mysterious about it.

The next hands were dealt and some of us examined the cards and some of us played blind. Every player placed a bet, every player upped the ante. After we played ourselves out, a fraction would return to work, a fraction would head to the next place on the list, and a fraction would head off with no declaration as to their respective destinations. Some of us held secrets larger and more dangerous than this, and for some of us this was our only secret. Some of us slept soundly at night and some of us could not sleep at all. We were all quite different.

We did the bad thing on the good leg.

We moved from the hand job to the blow job to the pussy job.

Often we were stunned by the monsters we had become, though some of us were not surprised at all.

What relieved us and comforted us the most was how normal we made each other feel.

And the girls, oh please, were normal too, their usual societal labels through usage and association so repellent and unfair that we always and only referred to them as either girls or women. Never, not ever, your labels.

Why can't you stop condemning them?

You want to see them all unfiltered. You are prurient or you want to withhold judgment until you hear our entire tale. You want us to be more window than mirror. What is it that you want?

But the poker was done and it was time for us to go. We split the bar tab equally regardless of who had eaten or drunk more or less. It was always our practice, always easiest, and we often chose the easiest practice of any endeavor. It was twenty-five a piece, including tip, a fair value. On the sidewalk in the frothy sunlight we said our good-byes with economy and warmth. Some of us descended into underground garages to retrieve our cars, some of us hailed taxis to our next appointments. Three of us started out on foot.

Among wealth, dominance, and accomplishment, which do you seek most avidly?

We were not particularly giddy, not particularly somber as we crossed the square to the street we sought, a repeat destination as a number of them were. It was one of our city's longest avenues, named after a famous local politician whose projects decorated our skyline, metal and glass spires looking eternally freshly scrubbed in our late spring sheen. We jostled along the street past cafés and restaurants, bars and shoe stores, and then up onto a brief overpass, over the train track out of our sprawling metropolis, and then down toward the waterfront, just down half a block more, where on the right was a muted four-story apartment building, and we pressed the button for the one location on the ground floor, and after a moment the door quietly clicked itself unlocked and we let ourselves in.

The walls of the corridor were black tile, the floors were marble. This was one of our city's finest neighborhoods, part of the Heights, that uphill swath overlooking our town between the mountain peaks and the waterfront. The corridor was silent, spotless, well lit. At the door to the apartment we paused, and it opened, sensing us waiting, sensing our greedy and yet restrained anticipation. The woman who let us in was our age—mid-forties—maybe older, her face an uneven complexion, her hair indifferently curly.

"Gentlemen," she said. "Good afternoon. Won't you come in?"

"Yes, thank you."

We entered and she shut the door quickly behind us. Underfoot was the same spotless white marble of the public corridor. To our right was a long counter or sideboard. At the end of the short hall were two doorways, one closed to the left, and the one directly ahead populated by two heavy-set women on swiveling office stools, their backs to us, chatting happily. We followed our hostess downstairs, along another marble corridor, to a room with its door ajar. Inside were a king bed with a copper-colored leathery spread and three steps that led up to a large whirlpool.

"Wait here and I will send the girls in. And, gentlemen, what would you like to drink?"

"Still water."

"Sparkling water, please."

"Rum and pineapple juice, thank you."

We were too shy for all three of us to sit at the foot of the bed; one of us stood to either side.

"How much is it again?"

"Four hundred a half hour, four-fifty for forty-five, five hundred an hour. Greek is a four hundred supplement."

"That's a lot for Greek."

"Geez, I've got to get my kids at school in thirty-five minutes."

"Then it's a half hour only for you."

We laughed.

Soon there was a knock at our door, perhaps it was timid, perhaps it was delicate, perhaps it was thoughtful.

"Come in!" we called out at once.

The door opened and the first walked in, the usual petite figure striding expertly atop black high heels, black thong underwear and black bra immediately apparent through a gauzy black knee-length gown, a sly smile composed on her otherwise neutral face though there appeared to be a glint of amusement in her eyes, her black hair shiny and yet softly hanging to her shoulders. She kissed us one by one on the cheek, stretching for those of us who stood and bending down for the one of us on the bed. "Sonia," she said, and turned and paused briefly on her way out to show us her other advantages.

"Perfect," one of us said.

The door shut and we all sighed. At least one of them was good.

The second knock was briefer; the parade had begun. She wore a white bikini top and black bottom, not a thong. Her hair was blondish red and she wore flats. "Gentlemen!" she said. She kissed us each briefly, but more forcefully or enthusiastically than the last. "Vanessa," she said. She turned and we could see the drawback or the attraction, depending on your taste. None of us said anything. She closed the door behind her.

"Too big."

"Too bad."

"She did have some nice qualities."

We could hear the heel-steps of the third approaching. We fell quiet. The faintest shade of grimness or potential relief had descended. We didn't know if there would be enough now, and we'd neglected to ask how many there were.

She was Asian and giggly, which we liked. She kissed us each playfully, employing a bit of tongue, which was relatively unusual. "Sophie," she said. "No; Claudia."

"Just make up your mind," one of us teased her.

"Claudia," she said firmly, and left laughing, her hand cutely covering her mouth, the door closing and then popping open an inch or two.

"Funny."

"Cute."

There were four or five more, of various sizes and colors, and we were trying to keep track. Some places left you a little notepad, but not this one. It could be terrible to make a mistake, but too many of them were wearing black, and every name ended in a vowel, and you had to develop a list of three because we hadn't yet figured out who would choose first. The hostess returned.

"Have you decided?" she asked.

Although it was not unusual to make no choice and then abstain, obviously it was not the preferred decision on anyone's part—not on our part, not on the host's part, not on the girls' part. It wasn't awkward, but it was . . . disruptive. Slightly disconcerting? Something like that.

"You go."

"No, you."

"He can go. I don't care. I'll be fine either way."

"Claudia."

"Amelia."

"Sonia."

"Thank you, gentlemen." The hostess nodded with a smile. "One of you can stay here. The others please follow me."

In our separate rooms our respective girls arrived, negotiated the duration, accepted payment, and returned with the drinks. We were showered or bathed. We were scrutinized for any imperfections and scrubbed accordingly. Then they washed. On the steps from the bath were carefully folded slip-proof mats. We toweled dry. The beds had been covered with fresh sheets. The sealed wrapper of a single prophylactic reflected near the far pillow. We lay down.

"Now you just relax."

"Now you can go to sleep, baby."

"Honey, what would you like?"

Compare creativity and wisdom. Which do you think is more important to possess?

We talked. Or we did not say a word. Or we gave some direction. We were active, passive, or somewhere in between. We had no idea what we wanted or we wanted it all or there was something in particular that we had to have. They shared our language or they spoke it well enough or what they spoke we could not understand and had to intuit. There could be a lot of gesturing and sometimes there was misunderstanding, and if so, we proceeded cautiously. We wanted to do what we wanted to do, but nothing was worth making them anxious. Imagine being them. Imagine entering a room and not knowing what you were going to get. Of course some places utilized panic buttons or intercom systems or the speed dial of a handy cell phone. Perhaps there were even taps in the rooms or other kinds of surveillance. But it is hard and not hard to imagine being them. We too were afraid at first.

At first.

At first.

At first this was something most of us would never consider. The words—the labels—themselves were so off-putting as to make it all entirely unimaginable. The culture in its cinema and television and theater summoned for the most part vixenish or victimized women and creepy or abusive men. The heart of gold scenario seemed as far-fetched as possible. And let us not speak about *Pretty Woman*. We not only abstained from the professionals, it wasn't for most of us even a possibility we were conscious of.

Years passed. We grew up, we married, we launched careers, we moved from place to place, job to job, we had children, perhaps on a business trip to an exotic locale we experimented once with a paid scenario, perhaps we had affairs, we progressed in our trajectories. And then, one by one but in the same short stretch of time, through our wives and the children's soccer league we grew acquainted in this intoxicating, vibrant, frenetic, absorbing city with its twenty-seven museums and thirty-four parks and beautiful waterfront and subterranean mall and ninety-eight brothels. We did not even know about the brothels. What we knew about were the vixenish or victimized women who clawed at us as we walked the main avenue late at night. What we knew was the frightening wizardry of their approach, the wild beseeching look in their eyes, the forcefulness of their fingers and hands as they tried to latch onto us or grope us. We would be coming home from poker or a bar, and they'd stand in packs of three or five, and they were never hesitant, and we were always scared, shy, appalled. They dressed almost like urchins, they lived we knew on the other side of the main avenue, in the Depths, and often you could see their keepers glowering over them like penitentiary watchtowers. We jammed our hands in our pockets and kept walking.

And then.

And then, as part of a desire to bond the husbands of this group of women who happened to be friends, our wives just this past winter organized a "field trip" for us to a distant southern city. It seemed at first unnecessary to us to fly away somewhere in order to get closer to one another, but a dozen or more of us signed on anyway. The wives provided us each with a guidebook and a carefully planned itinerary of museum stops, a harbor boat ride, a distillery visit, and a guided Segway tour. Dinners and lunches were arranged at some of the city's most highly regarded restaurants. It was a two-night affair, with little time for rest, each day ending at midnight and the next commencing at 8:00 AM.

We landed in gloomy, rainy, still cold weather. Many of us had not had time to read the guidebook or more than glancingly familiarize ourselves with the itinerary—after all, we were busy men with families and jobs—but each of the taxi drivers who took us into the city made it clear to us what the chief attractions were: horse-racing, whiskey, casinos, and a tightly controlled, twenty-four/seven red light district. Most of us professed little interest in the last element, but all of us admitted to substantial engagement in at least one of the other diversions. The mood in the air lightened considerably. Sure we would partake in a fair share of culture, but we would also enjoy a little decadence. We left our luggage at our hotel and marched out to lunch. We drank more than we needed to, and then it was agreed by two or three of the guys that on the walk back to the hotel we should pass directly through the district. The vast majority of us—nine or ten—reluctantly followed.

"But don't you see," a finger pointed at an unfolded

colorful sheet of paper, "it's even identified on the official tourist map."

It was not that we didn't or couldn't see it; it was just that instinctively or even quite consciously we wanted no part of it.

And there it was, in bold capital letters, RED LIGHT DIS-TRICT, the way our own new city identified CONTEMPORARY ART MUSEUM or OLD PORT or INTERNATIONAL ZOO.

By the time we arrived at the outskirts of the district, the uneven cobblestone streets had made our knees and backs ache, and few of us were in the mood to prolong the journey.

"Just take us the most direct way through, please."

"What is it exactly that we're looking for, anyway?"

The few savants who were slowly revealing themselves laughed heartily.

"You'll see."

The apparent main street ran along a picturesque inland waterway. Other than a few scattered sex shops, there ap-peared to be mostly bars and grimy takeout restaurants.

"I don't see anything," someone muttered. "And I'm fuck-ing exhausted."

"Look there!"

Up ahead, at the last building on the left, just before the district apparently ceded to a conventional redbrick and white-shuttered neighborhood, were three or four doors or windows emitting a pinkish glow.

"Come on!"

The pace quickened, although some of us dragged our feet, unsure, not wanting to know, anxious, perhaps even a bit concerned for our safety. When we all caught up with each other we were standing outside four lighted glass doors, two at street level, one four steps below, and one four steps above, a quaint diamond configuration. Behind each glass door a woman leaned or posed, dressed in a bikini or scant lingerie. One flicked a tongue at us. Another kept opening and shutting her door, a hand reaching out, beseeching us to join her. A third filed her carefully coated nails. And the fourth calmly surveyed the dozen of us, decided something about us, pulled up a stool, and sat, looking truly bored. The girl who kept reaching out for us popped her head out.

"How much?"

"Two hundred for twenty minutes," she said. "Like everyone else."

"It's the same price everywhere?"

"Of course. Are you coming in or not?"

Some of us edged forward, and some of us backed away.

"How many of us will you do at once?"

"Oh come on, dude," one of us said, "there's no need to talk like that."

"Lighten up. He's only joking."

"Three," she said. "But it's still two hundred for each."

"Will you take it up the ass?"

"I sure won't. But I'll put something up yours."

This was almost unbelievable, or maybe it was funny. Maybe it was even seductive. It depended on who you were. It was three o'clock on a wet, cold afternoon. You could see soggy firewood clumped at the door stoops.

"Time to head back, guys."

"Thanks, babe."

"Don't mention it," she said. "I hope one or more of you return." She shut herself again behind the glass door.

"What did you think?"

"Pretty traumatic."

"Oh, it was nothing. She was joking."

"I liked the one on the right side."

"You're nuts."

"Man, could we just get back to the hotel?"

We crossed a charming eighteenth-century stone bridge to the other side of the waterway.

"There have to be more."

"Are you sure this is the road back?"

"Just a minute, just a minute."

Abruptly we turned onto a side street. It was quiet and still and narrow, and men were positioned along it. To either side were pinkly lit glass doors, and in them, we saw, were every kind of woman, every color, every shape, every size, none wearing more than a swimsuit, all of them eyeing us or talking to each other or doing nothing in particular at all except standing behind their glass silently, indifferently. Men moved purposefully from door to door as if they were in a library hunting for a particular book. We stayed close together. Inexorably we stepped down the street. When we reached the end there were sighs of relief, sighs of exhaustion, sighs of panic, sighs of contempt, sighs of dismissal, sighs of eagerness. It was a collective symphonic outrush of breath, like we'd all been holding ours. We turned right and then turned right again, and it was as if we were entering the same pink street. There were the same types of carefully placed silent men, some ragged looking, some reassuringly diminutive, and there were the same kind of women all in some stage of near undress, and there we were, apparently caught on a conveyor belt that would not let us go, enduring or enjoying the second leg of a circuit of unknown distance.

"Are you all right?'

"Fine. And you?"

"I'm okay. What do you think?"

"How the hell do I know what I think? I feel sad for them."

"They don't look sad."

They looked bored, worried, distracted, mildly enticing, deceptive, overly playful, sinister, mindless, contemplative, ironic, harried. Maybe one or two were beginning to look attractive.

"We should be heading back."

"Yes, can we please get back?"

"In a minute. In a minute."

Time was becoming extremely important. It was all measured in time. How long could you look? How long could you resist? How long did you need? How long could you have?

"I think we've seen enough."

"Can you ever?"

"This is a downer."

"Give it time. Give it time. Don't overthink it, and don't prejudge."

Maybe you don't want to think or judge. Maybe you just want to see.

They were petrifying. They looked at you, and you imagined they saw you in all your potential squalor and sin, and you felt as if you would turn to stone and your dick would fall off. And if it didn't and if you did what you had no intention of doing, then certainly somehow and deservedly your dick would fall off. It was all about your dick and it was all about it falling off. And there they stood behind glass, wearing so little to show as much as they could, in such chilly weather you wondered how they kept warm, assessing your own capacity for commerce.

"At two hundred they're practically giving it away."

"I hear it's even cheaper for locals."

"Aren't we ever going to the hotel?"

"I'm getting a taxi."

"I'm with you."

"Guys, guys. We're going, okay? Just keep your pants on."

We all kept our pants on.

Later, at night, when we were full from dinner and a bit sleepy, and the restaurant was far from the district but close to the hotel, within walking distance, we climbed tiredly but determinedly into three cabs. When we arrived we got out; we knew where we were going. The narrow, pinkly lit streets were more crowded with men than earlier, yet still hushed. We walked more slowly and were now able to breathe as we walked, nearly familiar with all this as we were, and we chatted in somewhat low voices, and we lingered in front of glass doors unintimidated or trying to be unintimidated, and some of the women reached out and touched us, and some jokingly tried to pull us in, and some happily flaunted themselves behind glass, and some now looked at us with greater interest because they recognized us and they understood that we had returned. Some of the doors had curtains drawn across them and it was presumed that inside the inhabitants were otherwise occupied. Some of the doors were lit but empty, as if the girl couldn't be bothered to show her face or perhaps she was in the bathroom. Once or twice we saw two girls together in one doorway talking, and we assumed that one had temporarily left her station in this particular arcade. We walked the entire display and then we walked it again. We looked at each other and shrugged. We looked at each other and winked. We looked at each other and shook our heads and sometimes you could sense a deep sadness from some of us, but most of all there was a lot of ambivalence and ambiguity amidst this abundance. Would anyone go first? Did anyone want to? Why ever had our wives sent us to a town that had this? We were husbands, family men, businessmen; some of us betrayed our wives with lovers but all of us had expressed real affection for our spouses. We were all fathers with kids in elementary school, for god's sake. Could nothing stop us?

Before we commenced our Segway tour after the museums and lunch the next day, our guide looked at us and said, "And of course, gentlemen, I will take you through the red light district." Was there a more endearing sight than a dozen forty- and fifty-year-old men gamely maneuvering their Segways over uneven cobblestone? We bumped through colonial neighborhood after colonial neighborhood, each street more charming than the next, the houses monotonously quaint with their redbrick fronts and white shutters and black roofs, our guide narrating the history of everything we saw, a history of exploration and production and rebellion and independence and the evolution of humanitarian values. As we entered the red light district he said, "And this is the red light district. The girls are unionized and consider themselves self-employed, independent contractors. The fees are uniform. They rent in eight-hour shifts the doorways and attached rooms. This was all decriminalized thirteen years ago."

"How do they ensure the girls' health?"

"What do you mean?" The guide looked insulted.

"I mean, are they clean?"

"Of course they are clean," he snapped. "They're as clean as any of us. They're tested, just like anybody takes tests. And they use the protection you would imagine they use."

We motored onward, as the silence of the district built around us. We could hear ourselves whispering across the squeaky wheels and brakes.

"Independent contractors, he said. Self-employed, he said."

Our second—and last—night we again spent surveying the transparent lit doors. Warily we watched each other, waiting. In pairs we dropped out into taxis, professing fatigue or the need to pack or a late-night business call back at the hotel. Soon we were just four or five wandering among the pinkish doorways, inspecting, theorizing. Some of us had favorites—we liked the bottom one in the diamond configuration, or the black-haired one between the two blondes on the left side of the third street— and we would guide the others there and the girls would look up in anticipation and even hope until they saw it was only us, and then they seemed to know something about us that we hadn't yet recognized, that we wouldn't, that we couldn't, that at least on this particular night we simply weren't going to. At last we went into a nearby bar, where shadowy men hunched over beers. The air was acrid, nearly suffocating in its bitter still-ness. When two of us took off our gloves and placed them on the counter beside us, a stranger darted over and reached to snatch them and we had to put them back on.

"Nasty place."

"One beer and we're out of here."

It was already nearing two o'clock, and we were too exhausted or distracted to speak.

"Interesting trip."

"Very interesting."

"I had fun."

"Oh, I did too."

We dragged ourselves back to the hotel and up to the floor that held our rooms. We said our good-nights, and from behind our walls we strained to hear if anyone was making a move back out into the night. In the morning, on the plane, as we looked one another in the eye and saw the unfulfillment or the innocence, we could tell no one had.

"It's a good trip when you can go home and hug your wife and know you've got nothing to hide. That's not always the case, you know."

"I know."

Even before the plane landed some of us were muttering or joking about the need for a return trip, that we had wasted an opportunity. We were all businessmen of one kind or another, and we didn't like to waste anything.

"We should have done it. At two hundred I'm telling you they're practically giving it away," one of us mourned yet again.

We didn't know each other well enough. There was no trust. While we might have already confided certain dalliances and rendezvous, it was still a leap to take on something like this in front of each other. We wanted to minimize exposure. We hid from one another for weeks.

Soon we went out for drinks in our fashionable city, and then, before we really knew what was going on, two of us were in a cab heading to a place that one of us knew. "It's in an old apartment building in the garment district. I was taken there weeks ago by a friend, but the woman said all the girls were busy."

"All the girls were busy? That's a good sign."

The cab dropped us on a dark street with bleak remnants of the last snowfall. We hurried to the building and rang the bell. There was no answer. We rang again and again.

"I guess it's closed."

"Nuts."

We sat in a bar around the corner and watched the cold rain dribble down the front window.

"When were you there last?"

"In the afternoon."

"Maybe it's an afternoon place."

We met again the next day for lunch, the two of us. We were committed to keeping it quiet. We ate quickly, distractedly. We ate as if we had a plane to catch. We drank and it made us want to skip the rest of the meal. Within minutes we were ringing the bell at Number One Hotel. We were buzzed in and took the elevator to the second floor. A brown door at the end of a threadbare corridor had a gold plate with Number One Hotel on it. We rang at the door. A woman answered. She was our age, maybe a few years younger or older. She wore jeans and a loose-fitting shirt. There wasn't anything attractive about her and she made no effort to look attractive. She looked at us wordlessly, her eyebrows raised.

"We're looking for . . . uh . . . girls?"

"Of course. Come in, gentlemen."

We were escorted past a front desk into a small sitting room with worn floral wallpaper.

"Sit down and I will send them in."

"How much is it?"

"Four hundred for a half hour."

"What do you get for four hundred?"

"You get whatever you can do in a half hour, gentlemen." She smiled just barely and shut the door.

"Is that good?"

"It's okay."

"Wasn't it two hundred for twenty in—"

"Everywhere is different."

"Okay."

"You look a little nervous."

"I've never done this before."

"It'll be fine. I'll keep an eye out, I promise. I won't leave without you."

"Thank you."

The door opened with a mild knock and the first girl stepped into our little sitting room, kissed us both briefly. "Alba," she said, and turned. She had long black hair. She was small where she needed to be small and big where she needed to be big. In this light at this time of day after a few drinks she was terrific.

The second girl wore braces and was very thin. The third was heavier than she should have been. It is hard to recall the fourth. The woman our age returned.

"Well, gentlemen?"

We looked at each other.

"Go on."

"Alba for thirty minutes, please."

"And you?"

"I don't know. Are there more?"

"There should be in a few minutes."

"I'll wait, then." We turned again to one another. We'd been concentrating so hard we hadn't truly acknowledged each other. "You go on in. If I'm not here when you're done, then I'm in one of the rooms and you can just wait for me here. Okay?"

"Okay."

"Gentlemen, anything to drink?"

"No thank you."

"No thank you."

Would we always be such good clients? Would we always be so polite? It was hard to imagine what we'd always be.

It is hard to remember everything from this first visit just six months ago. The room was not as small as it could have been. A new shower stood like a wardrobe beside a sink, and a fresh linen spread covered the bed. Once inside, she very carefully and expressly locked the door. It is easy to recall the uncertainty, the fear. What would happen and how would it happen? Why did she lock the door? She undressed her client and then herself—how marvelous that inaugural inefficiency.

"Do you want a massage?"

"No."

She gave an easy grin. "Okay, then."

You were conscious of the way she put the condom on you with her mouth. You were conscious of how she had no problem looking you in the eye. You were conscious of the late winter daylight pouring through the exposed upper quadrant of the single window. You were conscious of the fact that you could have everything you wanted and, like the mechanical person you had become over the years, you proceeded through your preferences, and when you were finished and nearly alone on your side of the bed, she reached over and gently patted your arm and said in a gentle, veteran way, "Okay? It's about time to go."

"Okay."

You both got up and got dressed on your separate sides of the bed.

"Ready?"

You nodded and she picked up the phone by the door.

"We're ready," she said.

You waited until you could hear someone coming down the hall, a light knock on the door, and then you were allowed out into the corridor. Alba went one way and the hostess led you the other.

"Was everything okay?" she asked.

"Very okay," you said.

You were glad to see the waiting room just as you had left it. At some point in time you had paid at the front desk; you later learned it was always *before* at every place you had ever been since, so it must have been *before*. We went out the door, down the stairs, and into the waning daylight. As we walked along the bustling street, trying to explain and describe so many things, the insights and events crisscrossed each other like two vehicles traveling in the same general direction but on distinctly separate yet frequently intersecting roads. Nothing could be untwined from anything else, and nothing seemed the same. You were aware that you had done this. You were aware that out of all the things you had done, you had done this now, too. You felt relieved and disappointed at the same time. You felt a lightness and a despair. Somehow it seemed less grave than other things you had done, and somehow it seemed more serious. At least you would not have to worry about her. That was finished as soon as it was done. That was a segment of time that had no future or past, and yet it seemed to reach into your past and your future like a creature with sinuous limbs. The conventional part of yourself was appalled and yet allowed the absent presence of the woman somehow to grip you. She lurked on your hands and on parts of your body as if this had not been only a business transaction. Late at night as you lay in bed next to your distant and dozing wife, a voice in your head uttered, whispered, said, Alba, Alba, and you tossed and rolled and could not shut it up, until finally one day quite soon after no lunch but certainly a few drinks, we went back.

"Same drill as last time, captain. Except this time if I don't see something I like, I'll wait for you across the street on the bench there. Okay?"

"Okay." We were already ringing the bell for Number One Hotel. "And thank you."

"Don't mention it."

There was the same hostess and nearly the same parade, although Alba made a show of recognizing you and she was clearly, from your vantage point, still the best and the only. When the hostess returned you immediately offered her name, without waiting to be asked. Briefly we were alone in the waiting room.

"Well, captain, as you can see, again I have found I cannot make a choice."

"I'll see you soon."

"Yes you will."

"Thank you."

Again there was the payment to be made at the front desk, again there was the same fairly generous and well-lit room, again the door was locked. This time you disrobed yourself. This time you landed eagerly—not hesitantly—on the bed. She started with her mouth. A phone rang. It was her cell phone. It rang and rang.

"One second," she said.

She answered her phone and reached back with her free hand and gripped you. This was not good but she'd only be a second.

"Yes, this is Hotel One," she said. "Yes, we're open now. You can find us at the corner of ____ and ____."

She continued stroking you as she listened.

"We can do that," she said. "We can do all of that. You and your friends will be certain to have a most pleasurable time with us."

She listened and you began to notice your watch, a watch that had been bought for you by your family for a milestone birthday. A second had become a minute. She responded to the caller with further assurances and what you could characterize as a sales pitch. Two minutes. Three minutes. Four minutes. You were beginning to feel upset. This was your time. This wasn't right. At five and a half minutes she finally hung up. You couldn't really look at her. She took you through your preferences and you felt her and examined parts of her body, but you made sure you did not find her eyes. Who cared? She certainly didn't. Still you managed to get to where you needed to be, where you wanted to be, where the whole point of this was, if you were going to be honest about it. She smiled at you.

"Let me give you my number," she said. "That way we can make sure I am available whenever you want to visit."

When she tried to let you out of the room, she had to call and call. It was clear the hostess had left her post; perhaps she was at lunch. You imagined Alba was now in charge, and she'd had no choice but to answer the phone when she did. Everyone needed the work. Everyone was desperate. A strange woman—the cleaning woman?—finally came to escort you to the front door. Down and out across the street a cold sunlight fell over the slatted green bench.

"So how was it?"

"It was truly awful. She took a phone call, for god's sake. For five minutes right in the middle she took a fucking phone call."

"I hate when that happens."

"I sure did."

"I was worried when you ordered the same one, that I would have to go in and fuck her to get you some necessary distance. Now I can see that isn't a problem."

"Never again."

"Good for you."

We had a quick drink. It was hard not to be dazed and numbed by everything.

"Now what do we do?"

"We find another place somewhere. The inventory there is limited anyway."

"Maybe this is it for me."

We both laughed.

"Maybe."

Things were either spiraling out of control or settling down, it was impossible to tell. We'd heard of some other places but we didn't know or couldn't recall where they were. It was spring and the city was warming up and filling up at the same time, as if some imaginary gate to the outside world had suddenly opened and let in the curious and the frantic. As always at this time of year, the streets seemed to vibrate with sex. The women appeared to dress in as little as possible, each week shedding another layer of modesty and confinement, perhaps willingly objectifying themselves for the men, who openly examined them in ways that were clinical or voracious or both. Their jeans seemed to be painted on, and before long they were traipsing in diaphanous slip-on dresses that they could slip off, if only their desires were piqued. We would be heading to or from poker, to or from a bar, and our mouths would fall open at the sight of them, waves and waves of women. We had all lived a lot of different places and we had never seen anything like it. The bestselling T-shirt was a pictogram of our city's biathlon: Drinking and Screwing. It was the city where everyone wanted to be. It was the city where everyone was.

One evening ten of us met for poker at one of our houses, and afterward we went to a bar, and after that one of us said—one of us who had not been able to make the field trip south—this one of us said, "I know a place. You won't be disappointed."

Five of us begged off. Five of us stole into two cabs and headed toward the hills. Just after the long wide boulevard that traversed the city, we were let off at a simple well-lit door that said above it only *Girls*. A doorman in a black suit frisked us one by one, his hands as big as baseball gloves, and then let us in. A cashier said, "That'll be eighty each, gentlemen, but it does include a drink."

Somewhat surprised at the size of the fee, but dutifully, we paid.

Up eight steps was a long, large rectangular bar, and around it, individually and in groups of two or three, maneuvered, lounged, lingered, smiled forty or so women, each only slightly more modestly attired than the women in the pinkish door-ways in the southern city that you would in light of this latest discovery very soon nearly forget.

We plowed past the women and sat at the far end of the bar. There were some men, too, men like us yet not like us at all, older men, defeated men, unclean men, but so few and so engulfed by women that it was hard to spot them. Immediately from all sides women converged, exactly five of them, to match our number.

"Buy me a drink, honey?"

"Do you want to go in the back, love?"

"Come on, dear. What do you say?"

We looked at one another, wild with surprise and joy and fear.

"I've been here a few times," it was explained. "I bring my clients here. Believe me when I say it helps the business."

It was clear as we listened to the girls' accents that none of them were from here.

"Where are you all from?"

"Romania."

"Ecuador."

"Colombia."

"Brazil."

"Wherever you want me to be from, honey."

We all laughed. They were touching our hair, tickling our necks. Their fingers traced our arms and boldly moved wherever they felt like going, and they felt like going every-where. Their bodies turned this way and that, and we were urged to look and assess. They backed their way between our knees and sought what was driving this whole bargain.

"How much?"

"Five hundred for a half hour."

"That's a lot."

"Oh come on," our temporary leader said. "I'll buy you one. The first one is on me."

"Sure it is."

"I mean it. You know you want the Brazilian."

We didn't know. It was hard to imagine. The place was filled with cigarette smoke, men were placed here and there around the bar like rare pieces of furniture. It was all much more public than the apartment "hotel" on the corner of _____ and _____. You had never seen so many girls in one place wearing so little. It must have been like one of those frat parties you had never gone to, except it was all for sale and you could have any of them by merely saying, "Okay," or "It's a deal," or "I accept the price." The Brazilian's one-piece looked like it weighed an ounce, the Colombian's thong seemed more like a strand of string. Their bodies were toned and supple, and their smell when they leaned into you was subtly sweet and familiar.

"Come on, boys," one said. "Come *on*."

We were men in our forties and fifties, we were all mar-ried, we all had kids, we were all substantially to shockingly successful. We were all men of passion and indifference; even if we claimed a kind of unrestrainable desire, our ruthless and calculating qualities could allow us to control anything em-anating from within ourselves. Now we shook our heads or smiled sadly or just looked away.

"Come around again, okay?" our leader said.

"We'll see."

They clicked off down the bar, their heels like daggers growing out of their feet.

"They were good."

"Sure they were good. I told you you wouldn't be disappointed."

We traded in our receipts for a first round of drinks. We scanned the bar. There were so many girls there were even some we couldn't see, obscured by the island bar back. Some of them clung resolutely to the red banquette that lined the walls. Some of them worked the men on the stools. Some of them chatted in small groups. Occasionally through the din we could hear them laugh. They seemed to know each other. They seemed to like each other. A girl approached and asked for a coin for the jukebox, and one of us gave it to her. It was getting later than late.

"I'm out, guys. I'll see you around."

We were down to four. We drank, smiled, smoked, and welcomed and fended off various groups of girls.

"It stays open till four. We have plenty of time."

"Next round's on me, guys."

"Are you crazy? It's eighty a drink."

"I brought you here. At least let me buy you a drink."

The women kept coming and going like they were stuck in the same revolving door, and it was growing more and more difficult to remember whether we had seen any of them before and to recall their particular details. They felt us and we felt them. It was one, it was one thirty, it was two. We had children to get off to school in just six hours; in seven hours colleagues and clients and conference calls and patients awaited us. Right now in our homes and condos our wives and our sons and our daughters were asleep in the season between heating and air conditioning, the windows propped slightly open to allow for the occasional gentle breeze or the constant thin rush of air from the waterfront or from the hills. Our lives were large and full, warm with the continuous press of humanity. We all loved living here. Sometimes when we returned from business trips and vacations it was like returning from the land of gray and sepia to the city of Technicolor. Azure, mimosa, bougainvillea, cypress. A waterfront that was so intensely jade or turquoise or blue onyx or all three in wavering strips out to the horizon that you couldn't understand how it became so transparent when you cupped it in your hand. Women in black gauze, red satin, white silk crashing up against you and the rectangular bar found its feet and danced under your elbow and there before you glowing as if bronzed stood the most beautiful—

"Dude, are you okay? You seem to be fading, dude."

"Let's get him a taxi."

And even the taxi driver, when you saw her face caught by the rearview mirror, revealed herself to be such a stunning blonde that you waited and waited to learn her price, and this one you would take, this one you had to have.

"Eight seventy-five," she said.

You looked up shocked and hopeful and reeling in whether it was really going to be that expensive or that cheap, only to discover that you had arrived at your own cross streets. You paid and staggered from the car, trying not to slam the door behind you. Shouldn't everyone be for sale? Could even you, you wondered, as you fought with the outside door of your yellow stucco row house for possession of your own key, the damn lock refusing to surrender it, be for sale? No one would buy you, of course, a torn family man on the brink of fifty, but the idea of a world populated by equally accessible bodies intrigued, stimulated, and nauseated you. You turned this over in your mind as it seemed to turn you over—your wife, eventually your daughters and your son as they grew of age, all accessible in a global market of bodies. That was definitely not what you wanted. At last the lock gave up the key, and you entered, your home smaller than most. Past the playroom and storage room and up one or two flights of stairs (what was a flight anyway—an actual discrete set of stairs, or the unit of stairs from one floor to the next—you would have to look it up) to the kitchen and living room, also smaller than most. You silently turned the knob in the door and deftly let yourself in, immediately noting that she had left the sofa-side lamp on to help you navigate.

"So you're home," she said.

You tried not to look shocked or guilty. You'd done, after all, this time nothing wrong. "Hi," you said. "It went longer than I expected."

"It went *longer* than you expected? You were supposed to be home an hour ago. You have two feet. You could have left earlier."

"Yes," you admitted. "I just didn't want to be the first one."

"That's lame," she said, "and you know it." She returned to the open book on her lap. Her bare legs seemed as pale as bed sheets against the pumpkin fabric of the sofa. "If you don't want to come home, don't come home," she said from under the hood of her blonde hair.

"It's not that."

"Then what is it?"

"I've never had friends like these."

"That's for sure."

You saw the empty scotch glass perched on the cushion beside her. So at least she wasn't at her sharpest either, though certainly she was sharper than you. "What about you? You like your friends here better than anywhere else, too. It was your friendship that started it all."

"That's true. But I'm not out with them till three in the morning."

"Three in the morning?" You slapped your forehead. "I am such an idiot."

"You know what time it is." She sighed and shut her book and stood from the sofa and looked at you. She too was not unattractive. You were the only unattractive one you could think of. "Anyway, if you'd just come home when you say you would, that would help." She brushed past you toward the back rooms of the second floor of the row house. You'd long ceased saying good night to each other, though why this was the case you couldn't say. You both suffered from insomnia and perhaps you didn't want to jinx any chance you had.

"Flight," the dictionary in your hands said. "1. Escape. 2. Airplane journey. 3. A discrete set of stairs."

It was all an escape, it was all a journey, it was all discrete from the rest of your life, discrete and discreet, until one fine day when you would be found out. And then? And then?

The row house ticked around you, it was its own bomb waiting to explode in your face and blast you into the land of shame and isolation. You were sick, we were sick, we all seemed to be getting this bug, this incessant desire for pleasure without personal cost, for pleasure whenever and however and in whatever color and shape and tone we wanted. The swirl in the bar was the swirl in your head, and you looked at your watch and saw you had plenty of time until four, plenty of time to say fuck it and slip from the row house and slip from your real life for the sake of thirty minutes. Thirty minutes. Thirty minutes! You had your hand on the handle of the door to that world, calculating twelve minutes cab ride back, five minutes to cash in your entry receipt for a drink and slug it down, and still you had a cushion of some minutes in there. Who were you to think like this, vile, corruptible, despicable fraud! All for thirty minutes in some room you hadn't even seen yet, with one girl chosen from forty, for five hundred with about another one hundred and twenty in fees and round-trip fare. At least everything was divisible by ten. Ten was the number of adulterous encounters you had had back when that was as low as you thought you could sink. Why was everything attached to desire so immoral and contemptible and in tens? You disgust us. We disgust you. Tens!

So, how many of the *Ten* Commandments have you broken, and which of the seven deadly sins have you ever committed? Out of chastity, temperance, charity, diligence, patience, kindness, and humility, which do you practice and how frequently?

When you woke on the pumpkin sofa it was nearly six in the morning and you congratulated yourself on your restraint while of course admitting that you hadn't wanted to go back there alone and the mathematics of time truly had been too risky. You slunk off into bed with the her who was no longer a she but rather some entity you had contracted with for the business of running a family that you both had never known you'd wanted in the first place. You hoped for sleep and a sense of relief that you hadn't made the escape back to the girlie bar—*girlie* was okay, it wasn't like those other appellations which you would have no part of—but instead you lay with your eyes squeezed shut wondering when you could get back there.

We met one evening not far from this last one, on a street corner just above the great boulevard, between the Depths and the Heights, ironically—most ironically—closest to the homosexual quarter. We followed the sidewalk uphill half a block, turned in at Girls, were frisked by the doorman, paid our eighty each, climbed the eight steps to the bar, slipped the tender our tickets, obtained our drinks, and were consumed by women.

There must have been fifty of them this time, advancing in pairs because we were a pair, and while some of them were not our taste, we could honestly look at each other and agree: it was spectacular. Some all but topless, some all but bottomless (have you ever been to the bottomless club in _____; now there's an experience), some in practically nothing, all of them ravenous for work. It was a buyer's market, a market where only the drinks were overpriced. There were a blonde and a brunette who soon made themselves our favorites.

"Well, captain, I think, believe it or not, I have actually made a choice on this occasion." Her fingers were like tender cables, her lips collagenated certainly but not oppressively so, her overall line taut and yet willowy supple.

"I'm ready."

"Let's go, boys!" the girls said.

They led us around the bar and through a smoked-glass automated doorway behind which a remarkably fat lady waited at a cash register. A cash register!

"Will that be cash or credit?" she asked.

"Cash."

"Cash."

We paid, the girls retrieved their separate packets of sheets shrinkwrapped in clear plastic topped by a shinily-packaged prophylactic, and took us past the cashier down a hallway of many, many doors. We were Room Twenty-three and Room Twenty-five, right next to each other.

"See you at the bar afterward, captain."

"Yes, at the bar."

There was porn on the flat-screen TV, there was a separate bathroom with a shower, and soon there were fresh sheets spread over the queen-sized bed.

"Ah, you're married," the brunette said with a surprising disappointment.

"So tell me, are you married?" the blonde asked, with mild interest.

Even though we were in separate rooms, the answer was the same. Yes. Yes. Because what was the point of lying? Yet even though we told the truth, we were getting further and further from it. We proceeded regardless. Afterward, at the bar, on what would become many such occasions, we said things like *That one, she was my wife, since my own wife won't fuck me*, or *Hell, we haven't done it in months*, or *That was so good, I think I might just go home and fuck my wife*, or *I fucked my wife two nights ago so I'm in the clear for another five days*. We all had wives, and we proceeded regardless. Regardless?

Regardless. 1. Without regard. See *regard*.

Regard. 1. Concern. 2. Feeling. 3. Esteem.

We held each other in high regard but we operated without regard. We operated as if we were participating in some late night seamy reality sex television series that was not actually real, but was, to our minds, without consequence. What was happening to us? What was happening to you?

As our days unraveled and tied the five or six or seven or eight of us together in this adventure, it was revealed that some of us, while still new to this endeavor in our particular city, were old hands at this. Some of us were men who generally knew where to go in every port we found ourselves, men who could "order in" or "take out," men who had experienced the whole range from two hundred a crack, so to speak, to three thousand a crack, while others of us were so novice that even while we reveled in it, it devoured us and there wasn't a moment in time that we didn't wish we'd never started. Together we absorbed and analyzed the broad variety of venues, we sampled and shared the places and the women, meticulously comparing assessments while giving up nothing else about ourselves, not what we made at our businesses, not what kept us awake at night, not how we raised our kids or what we truly thought of ourselves. We were men, harmless men, dangerous men, regardless men. The friends we'd left behind in our native cities would perhaps not know us. We could not know each other, but we knew something so raw and true about one another that we were bound in a way that we could not fathom and did not dare articulate.

Five or six or seven or eight was a lot of exposure, and we watched each other like sharks for any sign of faltering. Six or seven or eight was, in the scheme of things, really too many. One was ideal, two was fine, three was okay, four truly the maximum. At heart we were mathematicians. Six was a lot of chance. Six was too many variables. The six words we dreaded most, the six words that would send us to the ledge, were words that could come from each other or our wives. Sullen words. Somber words. Accusatory words. Dangerous words.

I need to talk to you.

Words we would know instantly meant that somewhere somehow something had been dropped and someone who was not one of us had picked it up.

I need to talk to you.

No doubt despite our many acts of bravery—now that we had commenced in earnest, for example, our rule of never going it alone was being disregarded all over the place—we were cowards. Yet when we looked across the table over our poker or drinks, we didn't see each other as cowards. We saw each other as fools and adventurers and frolickers and assholes. We were six or eight ambitious and thoughtful men who had frankly investigated the arena of sexual activity and concluded that, no matter what, we had always and would always be paying for it, so why not pay for it the tried and true way, the way that was as old as storytelling itself. We did not have to justify ourselves to each other; all we had to do was keep silent.

"It's an addiction all right."

"Actually it's a proven biochemical condition. We're just guys who are hard-wired for this sort of thing and so we're being true to our internal infrastructure."

"Whatever it is, I'm loving it." One of us chomped furiously on his beer nuts. "I have never in all my life had this much fun, and I mean that."

"Fun is the only reason for doing it."

"That's for damn sure."

We were a band of happily unhappy men, intersecting with loci of women of multifarious moods and demeanors, of distant or unknown or fabricated countries of origin, their names themselves like islands: Ivonya, Isabella, Ellsandra, Angelika, Irma. Girls primed for the next date even when they were in the middle of your date. Girls who were human manikins of lingerie, ballerinas in bed, sensualists on six-inch stilettos. It never got old because there was always someone new, and it never was new because it was the oldest exchange of money for service in the world. Ivana, Iruna, Elizabeta, Isella, Isolda, Inge, Anna, Asa, Alba, Alicia, their names as exotic as the foreign countries they were purported to be from. Romania, Estonia, Latvia, Bulgaria, Russia, Colombia, Uruguay, Paraguay, Ecuador, Mexico, Guatemala, and the ubiquitous Brazil. They were never from here, never ever from here, their migration the first act of the transformation that awaited them at their destination.

Perhaps they'd answered ads, perhaps they'd always had such a plan, perhaps they'd wound up here by accident. Perhaps their names were real, perhaps they were not. Some of us liked to talk with them as if interviewing them for a job—where are you from, how long have you been here, are those clothes really yours—and certainly in each instance a particular job was at stake. Others of us liked to chat with them as if in pursuit, as if the outcome were not so assured. A few of us preferred to say nothing at all, perhaps not wanting to waste our breath, perhaps intimidated or shy, perhaps indifferent to or incapable of even the faintest conversation essential to seduction. Sometimes when you talked with them you felt as if your head were splitting open, because you knew that every word exchanged was a lie, and sometimes you tried to make up for this by insisting that you yourself told the truth. And sometimes you concentrated on them so intently that your eyes began to hurt because you were searching for a clue as to who they really were. We were a gang of men bonded by the secret enactment of our ordinary desires, and this was a world we entered knowingly, shocked at our own audacity and profligacy and hopelessness and immorality and utter tawdriness. Why, we asked ourselves a hundred times, a thousand times, why? Because we wanted to, and because it was on so many fronts so simple and so without resistance that the ease of it was like a drug itself. Perhaps this is what people of power found—that they could have anyone, take anyone—what Roman emperors felt, what dictators and kings felt. Perhaps it was that. But it was also more and also less. The acute secret among us created an unspeakable intimacy, the gravity of which made us feel as if we were engaged together in a great and horrific and mortal struggle. We excused ourselves with simple lines like *You always pay for it*, and after our escapades we told each other everything so that it became like we were telling each other nothing at all, but we understood that nothing could make up for what we had done and were still doing; even if somehow we managed to cease, we could not erase what we had already committed. And what we sensed from our group of indulgers was a fundamental ruthlessness. If we could do this, was there nothing that we wouldn't do? And if we could rationalize this, were we capable of rationalizing anything?

It was, in the final analysis, the damn Girls bar that made it so suddenly easy and very possible, so that we no longer bothered to resist any pull at all. We would call each other up and say, "Do you have ninety minutes?" or "Are you free for an hour or two later this evening?" and such terms were so minimal it was impossible to refuse. "I have six hundred burning a hole in my pocket." Or, simply, "Absolutely." There followed the slowest and quickest ninety minutes of your life, first constantly checking the clock on the wall of your living room, the TAG Heuer on your wrist, the bedside digital alarm in your child's room, for the countdown to your release, your escape, when you'd turn to your wife and say crisply, innocently, "Back in a little over an hour," and then you were out the door, down the stairs, and onto the street, rushing with as much dignity as you could muster to hail a taxi, carefully offering an address but not the exact address, meeting one of us just half a block or a block off target, moving with disguised pace to the establishment in question, and then, boom, you were there, shaking the hand of the doorman who, if he had the time, gave you a bear clasp and never frisked you again, not even when you raised your arms as if he might be sticking a gun in your gut. "Oh no, not you, sir," he laughed jocularly, his massive shoulders shuddering with mirth. "You are our dear client." And when you tired of the Girls bar, there near the end of the city's great urban avenue, the one named after the ambitious and visionary politician, awaiting your discovery was the Pink Pearl. The Pink Pearl.

This was the downstairs warren of ornate private rooms we have told you about, this was where each girl was only four hundred, only four hundred, and the drinks were free and you could go at any time of day or night, they broke only from eight in the morning to ten in the morning, to clean and have one of their shift changes, and so you knew exactly when to arrive if you didn't want to be stirring any milkshakes. This was the place where the hostess always asked you, "Anyone in particular?" and you always said, "No," and then the parade began. This was the one where every single girl eschewed the hood until you were ready to get on with it, where you were able to feel her naked mouth on you, where it often came close to GFE but of course never ultimately was, where four hundred was a bargain. Until you found the place for two hundred and fifty.

Two hundred and fifty. So close to the mythic two hundred of that southern city you'd all but forgotten. Two hundred and fifty, where there wasn't a single defining mark on the panel of buttons at the hulking front door of the cavernous old apartment building, and so you had to try all sixteen of them at once and then you were let in, and in the brightly lit entryway up the open flights of stairs that framed the ancient elevator shaft you saw on the third floor a great door opening for you. Two hundred and fifty. You could not believe your luck. We raced up the stairs two steps at a time. What a fine old building it was, as you, who had become our true leader, who found us new place after new place with your clandestine internet research, blinked your bright serious eyes in the surprisingly bright light of the foyer of the brothel, women walking to and fro, until we were taken to a fine old bedroom and the girls as in other places began to appear one by one. You liked the dirty blonde in the French maid's outfit. "What a cliché," you said, laughing at yourself, and you stayed in the room and waited for her, while we others were escorted to our situations. Two hundred and fifty. Afterward, at a bar down the street, you were morose—as you often were. "This one was different," you claimed. "It was." You paused, summoning yourself. "It was kind of clear she didn't want to."

"She didn't want to?" we said in disbelief. "You mean she had no enthusiasm, or she really didn't want to?"

"I think she really didn't want to," you said, staring at your rum and pineapple juice. "Maybe it's the two hundred and fifty."

"Mine was fine," one of us said.

"So was mine."

"Did she do anything in particular?"

"She did everything, of course," you said. "But she was definitely . . . sullen."

"Sullen?"

"Sullen." You swallowed a sip of your favorite drink. "She didn't smile. When she got undressed she immediately slid under the sheet as if she was trying to disappear. She didn't bother showering before or after. She shut her eyes."

"She sounds depressed."

"She was Russian."

"That might explain it."

"It's just not enough money."

"Probably not."

"So we won't go back."

"Okay, we won't go back, captain."

"Thank you," you said, and you continued staring into your drink, which was always too yellow and too sweet. We never understood your predilection for your damn rum and pineapple.

"I've never paid a girl and not followed through," you muttered.

"Of course not."

"I wish I hadn't this time."

"Lesson learned," someone else said.

"Oh shut up."

We could talk like that to each other and it didn't trouble us, that was how close we were.

"Another drink, captain?"

You looked at your watch. "Nope." You threw some money on the counter and the girl behind the bar smiled at you.

"She's cute, captain. Smile back."

"Screw you," you said, and were down the bar and out the door without so much as a good-bye.

"What's with him?"

"His girl didn't want to. He said she was sullen."

"Oh, I hate when that happens."

We all looked at the door as if expecting you to return.

"Suddenly, he's in agony."

"He was always the serious one."

"He'll get over it."

It was around this time that you began having trouble with your older daughter. She was sixteen and starting to become a woman. One Saturday as you and your wife sat over a leisurely coffee, she came bustling out of her room all dressed and ready to go. "Off rollerblading with some friends," she said on her way out the door. "Call if you need me." You looked at each other and thought aloud, *How odd.* She couldn't rollerblade and she never got up early on Saturday and she never even talked like that. An hour later she called and told your wife that she was stuck at an HIV clinic trying to secure an AIDS test, but they wouldn't give it to her without parental permission. Your wife raced down there while you watched the other children. You paced the apartment, stoking and throttling your ironic rage. "Dude," one of us would tell you later, the one who always said *dude*, "this is what being a parent of a teenager is all about."

"Dad," your daughter later said, "my business is none of your business."

Maybe your business was failing too. You were investing a fair amount in your pleasure and this pleasure was quashing your hunger and your hunger was essential to your success. Except for that one night, when the girl had seemed reluctant, you were probably too happy and sated to succeed any longer. It was also true that this was when the economy was beginning to suck. Sometimes in those days when we went to Girls we were the only guys in there. An Estonian girl told us that they were turning only five or six guys a night, and often those were us! We had never felt in such demand.

And then, without much warning, we caught an odd scent, a whiff of something we'd long been watchful for but up to now had not detected. There was a rumor going around, about the wives, about certain unfulfilled or unhappy or neglected or disenchanted wives. Perhaps they were our wives, perhaps they weren't. We saw it first on the sidelines of the soccer fields, the jauntiness of a new hair style, the self-possession that comes with being wrapped in the latest fashion, and it wasn't just in the clothes they were wearing, it was happening when they weren't wearing any clothes at all. You could smell it.

"What the hell is going on?"

"I have no idea, but did you see that?"

"Yeah, I saw it, and I don't like it."

"It's kind of hot."

"They're our women, for god's sake."

"And we're their men."

"That's precisely it."

There was a hint of them in even the circle of mothers finding new intimacies. There was a hint of them on the tony streets of our most exclusive and expensive shopping district, women in their forties and fifties moving with a renewed sense of purpose, a newfound vivacity, a certain exuberance and self-confidence in their step, women who'd suddenly rediscovered that they were indeed attractive, that someone somewhere indeed wanted them, women who were again getting some, and it wasn't from us.

"I'll hire someone."

"Me, too. I'll hire a whole goddamn team."

We put out word, we laid out cash. "I'm just not seeing it," you said. "She wouldn't."

"Sure she would."

"That guy over there." We nodded our heads at one of the soccer fathers. "He told me he found out his wife was buying lingerie and he wasn't getting to see any of it. He's having her followed."

"But he's not one of us," you said.

"Who knows," we said. "It doesn't matter. We just need to figure this shit out."

"You guys are nuts," you said, distracted as you were by that last time with the Russian and whatever the hell was going on with your business.

One night in your darkness you rushed out to the Pink Pearl by yourself. It was a Saturday, barely past midnight. Surely you had to know you'd be stirring the milkshake. You were shown into a room that didn't even have a bath and where the bed took up an entire wall. You should have left then. When the parade began it was so short that if you had blinked you would have missed it and unfortunately there wasn't anything to miss. Through the walls you could hear the exertions and exhortations of the competition that had beaten you to market. "Is that all there is?" you asked the hostess. "I'm afraid so," she said. You lay on the bed and stared at the dark ceiling. Could you really get up and leave? "Suzannah?" the hostess suggested. "Suzannah," you said, without even looking at the hostess and without even knowing which of the four Suzannah was.

When she arrived you wrestled to remember what we had tried to tell you to do if it went like this, that if you could just demonstrate some enthusiasm she would respond enthusiastically. She was a person, for god's sake, and you struggled to overlook her noticeable belly and the distinctive sag of her buttocks, but she saw you noticing. You took a long draw from your drink. You'd never had a drink for four hundred before, but that was what this was beginning to look like. You glanced longingly at the door out as you made your way into the shower. In the distance you could hear howls of ecstasy, but even your own shower offered only a lukewarm trickle.

"I can't believe this," you muttered to yourself.

As you were released from the room twenty-three minutes later, a beautiful girl in a red slip came staggering from quarters far larger than yours down the hall, wiping her mouth with the back of her hand while back inside the room a guy was thrusting himself into another girl who was on all fours atop a great wide bed, and as you took this all in you were dismayed to discover that all three of them were looking at you, wondering what the hell had led you to be standing there frozen in place. You hurried up the stairs.

Behind the third door on the first floor, a door you had failed to notice before, you could hear several showers going and the almost dreamy chatter of girls resting between gigs, talk of imminent vacations to the mountains or on the coast, of moving back to their hometowns and buying houses, of lazy husbands or inattentive boyfriends. You wanted to stand there and listen forever, to enter their ordinary lives, but there really was no place to linger. Outside, on the street, you lit a cigarette and began walking quickly down into town. Even a bad night could be a good night, if you gave it a chance. It struck you, much delayed, that the Pink Pearl, unlike all the other places you had been, had no locks on any of their private rooms, and that it was, from what you could see, staffed entirely by women. It was hard not to like the Pink Pearl, even when it gave you a less than mediocre girl. You got home quickly, these solo trips much more efficient than our garrulous camaraderie, and your wife cupping her scotch on the pumpkin sofa smiled warmly at you and said, "Hey, you're home early." You two hadn't had sex this entire spring. It wasn't fair for our wives, you said, to compete against eighteen- and twenty-two- and twenty-seven-year olds who had to make their living off their bodies. Our wives were beautiful enough, but not that beautiful, not that lithe, not so silky as professionals. Yes, we couldn't dispute the occasional whiff of the unsavory. Yes, we couldn't disagree that there were some things we certainly would not do with the girls, but the girls were still girls. They were not middle-aged women who had suffered through the wrack and ruin of childbirth and breast-feeding and whatever other corrosive physical duties child-rearing involved, and surely there were many. Whereas for us the only thing that childbirth took from us restored itself easily and almost instantly in our bodies, and for whatever other ills it created there was always the gym and the bar and these apartments and places that we had so recently discovered.

Despite what anyone might think, we did possess some empathy for our wives. We loved them, for god's sake. That wasn't enough, we knew, but it was true.

"Shorter walk than usual," you said.

She looked at you intently as you sat down beside her on the corduroy sofa.

"Are you having an affair?" She leaned closer to you and you made yourself not pull away. "You're having an affair, aren't you? I bet you're having an affair!"

"I am not having an affair."

"'Course you are." She gave you a strange, drunken smile, a lure as if to say *that's all right, I don't mind* when you knew she would mind a whole hell of a lot. She touched you playfully with a single index finger. "We have had sex just twice the last six months. So who is this you're having an affair with?"

"Whoever could I be having an affair with?" you asked.

You both thought about that for a minute. You could not afford to move from her, but you were curious to look into the liquor cabinet to see how much scotch she had drunk. Then you spied the empty bottle on the floor by the trash. You returned to making yourself look her in the eye.

"Don't know," she concluded.

"There's no one," you said.

"'Course there is," she said. "Maybe one of your clients. Maybe someone who pays you money," she teased.

You laughed genuinely. "Now that's rich," you said. You patted her on her bare knee and strode to the liquor cabinet. An opened bottle of scotch beckoned. So she'd had more than a few shots. That was a lot for her. You poured a substantial glass, hoping that might get you in the mood. Over the past few months and many girls, several fine conclusions had found their way to you, and one was that marriage was a most unnatural and misguided institution. Even saintly husbands confessed that they lusted in their hearts.

"Are *you* seeing anyone?" you asked, feeling the odd cocktail of hopefulness and dread as that mouthful left you, wondering if what we were trying to tell you could actually be true.

"Don't be ridiculous," she said. "Who would want to see me?"

You knew that at least one of us had a crush on your wife. We'd told you that. You also knew it was against all rules to pursue anything like that, unless it was agreed to by all parties, and while you hadn't disagreed you clearly hadn't agreed yet either. The truth was we were all hypocrites, outlandishly betraying our wives while being intensely territorial about them in the typical male fashion. It was a contradiction we refused to discuss.

"The tenor," you said, trying to keep the anxiety from your voice.

"Him?" she said, and gave that little toss of her head that she used when she was being flirtatious. "He's not interested in me."

"He should get his own girl," you said passionately, bitterly, because that was a line you'd heard one of us use to great effect. Talk about deflecting scrutiny, suspicion, whatever it was!

"He's harmless," she said.

"No one is harmless," you said.

She sipped her scotch. "Apparently not."

You both sat there on the sofa thinking about the tenor. None of us knew him particularly well, but he was always there, in the background, lingering, invited to everything but never hosting a thing himself. One of the kids' schools called him its singer-in-residence and he was in residence, all right. Our wives bought his cds and steered our children to him for singing lessons, but with the exception of dinner parties we wouldn't allow him in our homes. We had good instincts for this kind of thing. That tenor. That candy-assed tenor. There were worse guesses than that tenor.

"You like his vests," you said mournfully.

"They're silly," she agreed.

"It's a cliché to have an affair with a tenor."

"I'm not having an affair! You are!"

And so we all were fathers, brothers, sinners, betraying our wives, betraying our families, and betraying ourselves, and perhaps wondering if we too were being betrayed, but never betraying each other. If you relaxed and looked objectively enough, you could see the honor in this, though when we read or heard words like morality or character or soul, or love or trust or fidelity, or marriage or parent or father or husband, or truth or honesty, of course we cringed. It was awful to think that *we* were the men who made us feel normal, who allowed us to feel sane, because we were all as evil and hurtful as each of us was. Was there any way to reinvent ourselves and jettison from this moral catastrophe of our own creation?

"So tell me about this affair you're having," you gently commanded between sips of scotch. Your job, as you knew, your one and only job was to admit nothing because then the only thing left would be to hand over the keys, and you did not want to hand over the keys. It wasn't only about the keys, of course. It was about the finality that the keys would represent, as if—if it weren't for the fatal possibility of surrendering the keys—you'd really engaged in nothing definitive, nothing that had set you two apart forever anyway, nothing that had already irreversibly alienated you from whatever the fuck the so-called mainstream of society got to inhabit so fully and innocently.

"Oh bother," your wife said, quoting one of her favorite characters from one of those kids' books and draining the rest of her scotch. "I'm off to bed before I pass out. You coming?"

"Soon," you called after as she staggered toward the back room. "Pretty soon."

Now you were all lit up like some object of a firing squad, but there was no one to shoot you. You poured yourself another shot. With one admission you could change your life, but whoever wanted to do that? We were all better off and better at skillfully plotting a relatively blameless exit than daring the fatal bold admission. And besides, you had us to think about. By now we were engaged in a pattern of behavior with a distinct design and texture easy to discern if only one square were to reveal itself. You could not be that square. None of us could be that square. Even those of us with "tolerant" wives, wives who never interrogated or investigated, wives who declined to try to push us out on any ledge, wives who practiced willful ignorance, wives who simply looked the other way, even these wives would be forced to confront the facts of our betrayal. You went to the window and looked out. Outside in the great vastness of the city, tucked away but not out of reach, just waiting for you to find them, were the No-Tell Motel, the Do Come Inn, Kiss and Make Up, the Missionary Motel, the Get Lucky Hotel, the All in One Inn, Menáge à U. How long could this go on? How long would this go on? Why did we all stare into and out of windows all night? That glimpse you had this evening, that glimpse through the open door of the guy and the girl doggy-style on the bed, what did that look like? For her, it looked like *work*. Of course you'd already learned that there were girls who moved from town to town seeking more and more work like fruit pickers following the seasons. You'd already seen the girls who worked the bars with the aggressive polish and ease of car salesmen. You'd already understood that there were girls who desperately wanted to do this as much as anyone might desperately want to earn a living or keep a job. For god's sake you'd always known it was work for them. Even if there were girls who did this also for the fun of it, for the escapism, performance, and exhibition of it, as if they were actors in front of a camera or on a stage. Even if seemingly there were girls who might do this also for the essential intimacy of it, who actually wanted to cuddle with someone they didn't even know because they knew him in a way that perhaps nobody else—not even his own wife—knew him. They separated themselves, all these girls did; just like they had separated themselves from their hometowns, they were separating themselves when they were with us. From time to time we were certain their true selves had to catch up with them, but every night—or every morning, or every afternoon, or whenever it was that they were with us—their true selves had to be left behind. We knew a girl who chewed a wad of bubble gum through everything imaginable. We knew a girl who changed her name every month or every week or once every few days. We knew a girl who said she wanted to return home and be an accountant, and yet she couldn't add two three-digit numbers in her head. We knew girls who couldn't remember they'd been with us and we knew we couldn't always remember girls we'd been with. We knew girls who traveled with poppers and insisted we partake with them and we knew girls who wouldn't even so much as indulge in a sip of alcohol on the job. We knew girls who wouldn't kiss on the lips and we knew girls who couldn't help but stick their tongues in our mouths. We knew girls who had to parade in front of us as they undressed, and we knew girls who looked away as they took off their clothes and then slunk under the sheets as if they wanted

to hide. We knew girls who insisted they loved their jobs because they really did like "meeting new people," and we knew
girls who when asked on this same point answered *no* with
such stark simplicity it was nearly a turn-off.

"Soon," you muttered again, even though there was no
one there to hear it, even though you had your back to the
apartment and were talking out the window. You thought this
was easy? Of course it was easy; that's what made it so hard.
A mosquito landed on your forearm and you tried to shake it
off. It didn't budge. That mosquito. That mosquito wouldn't
know when it had had enough, it would keep coming back
for more, it wouldn't stop itself. Some mornings you'd killed
mosquitoes so engorged with your blood that they were more
you than they were themselves, the blood splattering in your
hand, tiny bubbles of it clinging to your palm like sticky orbs
of mercury. You looked hard at your new mosquito. The code
was to ruin only your own life, but that was impossible to
keep, because every second you were doing what you were doing; you were ruining someone else's life—the one astride or
under you, and of course the ones in your own family. That
word tore through you and in one deft gesture you set down
your wine glass and slapped the mosquito hard against your
own skin and felt the sting as your own blood escaped from it
only to be reabsorbed into your open pores.

"Daddy," a young and yet not young enough voice said
from the room behind you, "what are you still doing up?"

You wheeled and saw it was your sixteen-year-old, in her
T-shirt and boxer shorts, for once home earlier than you on a
Saturday night.

"Waiting," you said. "Thinking," you said.

"Uh-huh," she said, immediately losing interest, bending
into the fridge and fishing out a bottle of juice, then standing

and uncovering the top and lifting the open container and tilting back her head—

"Don't," you said.

"What?" She stopped herself.

"Germs," you said.

She looked at you patronizingly. "Sure, Dad." She pulled down a glass from the cupboard and patiently filled it with juice, turned and held up the glass for you to see. "Happy?" she said.

"You are such a little—" You stopped yourself. The hypocrisy could be overwhelming at times, couldn't it?

"What's eating you?" She stood eyeing you as if she knew everything, and that was saying something.

"Never mind," you said. "Drink out of the bottle. I don't care."

"I got an A on my honors math test."

You grunted. "How are things with your boyfriend?" You liked the idea of tolerating her boyfriend and being able to talk about him better than the fact of tolerating him and having to talk about him.

She looked at you steadily. "They're fine, Dad. Just fine. How are things with you?" She leaned lazily against the kitchen counter, sipping her juice, and it appalled you how she seemed to be in the position of authority. Sometimes you just wanted to tell her everything, confess it all, because she seemed like she might really get you and you were eager to learn her reaction; somewhere in there might be a revelation for you, something to lead you out of the unspeakable mess you had created and were building on every day of your godawful existence.

"Can we just cut the crap?" you said. "I mean, if we don't have anything to say, we don't really need to talk with each other."

"That's lovely, Dad." She slammed the glass in the sink. "I'm so glad you love talking to your oldest child." She turned on her heel and went down the hall.

You stood there in the living room looking at the spot she'd vacated in the open-plan kitchen, the mosquito's blood or your blood drying on your forearm. While some of us would argue that we were natural fathers, you were not. You didn't know how to talk with your children and you didn't know how to play with them either. You were too self-aware. When you were with them you had this constant feeling of being outside yourself, watching yourself with them, observing, evaluating, speculating. God you ought to just go to bed. Why didn't you just go to bed? All this accusation and inclusivity, and yet you're left with only separation, the you who is not you, the you who is outside of you, the you who can't or won't believe who you have become. We had to deny anything and everything and we were full of denial. What you'd wanted was to get laid. What you'd always wanted was to get laid. Even when you were getting laid you wanted to get laid. You once read something somewhere about a man who for his age—fifty?—thought that by paying a girl once a month he'd solved the problem of sex rather well. But you knew the problem of sex could never be solved, even when you were having it all the time. Everyone just needed to know who they were, but you had fallen off that truck a long time ago. Not only couldn't you know anyone else, but you couldn't know yourself. It was too repellent, too repulsive, too revolting, too disgusting.

"Daddy?"

Now it was your thirteen-year-old girl standing there, as if the house itself had decided to offer you its own particular parade.

"What are you doing up, honey?"

"I couldn't sleep." The sad gangly waif labored over to you wrapped in her favorite blanket and you gave her the obligatory hug. It was disconcerting how their cuteness had to fade and you had to lose that physical connection you used to have for them when they were so small and sleek. You still loved them, of course; you just didn't feel like kissing them as much.

"You want some ibuprofen?"

She shook her shaggy head. "Already had it." She looked around. "What time is it?"

You knew without checking but you checked anyway. "Three fifteen."

"Hey, are you bleeding?"

You both glanced at your arm. "Mosquito blood," you explained.

"Gross."

"Probably my blood, too, the way these things work."

"Grosser still." She grinned. "Can I have a glass of water?"

You went to the cabinet and yanked down a glass and pulled the good water from the fridge. She was thirteen and really should be getting her own water. In some cultures girls her age were just on the cusp of being introduced to the kind of thing that was tearing you apart. In some cultures so much was normal that it made you question the whole concept of normal. You gave your daughter the glass of water and tried to think of how safe your life was. The thirteen-year-old took great gulps of the water, as if she'd been dying of thirst or as if she couldn't wait to get away from you. What did you two ever talk about? Movies, music—you knew nothing of music, but she knew quite a bit. Once you picked her up from a school dance and asked her how it had been. "How was it?" she repeated. "It was only the best night of my life, was how it was. I slow-danced with a boy." And you felt yourself sicken, as if someone had stuck his hand inside you and squeezed your stomach. Now you reached over and tousled her hair.

"I'm going to bed," she said, handing you her glass and shuffling off. "Don't let anyone wake me."

Outside, down on the street, you could hear someone drunkenly singing. What was it?

We're all going to hell. We're all going to hell. We're all going to hell—so long.

We're all going to hell. We're all going to hell. We're all going to hell—so long.

You tried to look out to see him, but you were too high up or at the wrong angle. You drank from the glass in your hand. The cell phone in your pocket vibrated and you took it out. A text: Just had drinks in one of the usual places. Quite good. Missed you.

There was nothing quite like a coded message from one of us. You laughed quietly and erased it. Although it was now hours since what you'd seen through the open door at the Pink Pearl, you wondered if it had been one of us. It could have been. It could have been. And wouldn't it be so like us to get the better girls, more of them, and the better room? You turned off the phone and dragged yourself down the hall, past your thirteen-year-old's room where she was tossing and in obvious frustration, past the framed pictures of the family at holidays and on vacations, past your oldest's room where you could hear the easy regular breathing of certain sleep, to the open door at the end of the hall, where on his junior bed your five-year-old lay happily snarled up in his favorite blanket, blue with white rabbits, and on the headboard he had fastened a plastic mask of a mutant turtle. He'd claimed that it protected him at night, and you'd marveled at the ease and skill of the way he addressed his own particular terror.

In your room you sat on your side of the bed, at the foot of it, and began to remove your clothes. As you took off your shirt and saw your own naked belly you recalled as if for the first time where you'd been and what you'd done tonight. It was too easy a thing to forget. You weren't desensitized but you were, sadly, experienced. Not long ago you'd lost count and you'd lost track, so it was not even an actuarial exercise. You disagreed that it was an addiction. You wriggled from your pants and looked at your legs. You rarely looked at yourself. You were not that interesting. None of us, when you thought of it, were mirror guys, though we did not mind them in the back rooms and the basement quarters of our favorite establishments. When we went out, we dressed to blend in, usually earth tones, maybe an occasional red or bright blue. There were in our city, of course, also kidnappings and car bombings, and we had no desire to stand out. The very successful were always advised against both routine and ostentation. And the places we went, it was not like we were competing, for god's sake. Were we?

Perhaps we were. Perhaps we were.

You lay in your marital bed and waited for darkness to descend, but only a gray light that ever so gradually turned brighter, like someone slowly turning up the volume on a painfully familiar song, began to seep in from around the curtained outline of your window. It was another Sunday. You thought of your god; you hadn't thought about your god in a long time. You often wondered what your spiritual guy, a pushy needy man ten years younger than you, would have to say to you if he knew about you and what kind of absolution he could offer. Probably none. None sounded about right; maybe that was why you never went. You thought of Easter dinner with some of us, how we'd all come dressed from church, and how you marveled at our coiffed beauty, and how beautifully prim we all appeared, our wives with their powdered noses and pearl necklaces, our children in their saddle shoes or Mary Janes, their teeth freshly brushed and their hair slickly combed, and us in our Burberry ties and Armani sport coats. "My god, you're all gorgeous," you said, and your wife gave you such a sideways look because of course you were underdressed, you were still so resentful about the whole construct of religion.

Like him, we are all going to rise again, good friend. We are all going to rise again and be redeemed and all that. Just not now. But soon. Soon.

You woke in the late morning, more tired than if you had not slept, your son hanging on your foot, your wife eyeing you sternly. "Just what is your problem?"

"I can't sleep," you said.

"I know. But why?"

"I'm exhausted," you said. You tried to look at her but it was too bright. "What time is it?"

"Noon," she said bitterly.

It was always about time between you and her, wasn't it? It was always about time with all of us about every goddamn thing. Had you ever seen another group of men check their watches as much as we did?

"Look, I know it's your birthday, but we're due at the park in ninety minutes and no one is dressed and we haven't done any shopping for tomorrow morning or even dinner tonight. Could you please get up and help me?"

"My birthday?" You felt yourself smile. "I'd forgotten."

"There are gifts on the table," she said, her face colored with rage and something like love. It probably wasn't love, but it was close, close enough, far past what you deserved. You gently shook your son from your foot and levered yourself out of bed.

Down the hall, at the living-dining-room table and slouched on the pumpkin sofa, waited the sixteen-year-old and the thirteen-year-old.

"Happy birthday, Daddy," the sixteen-year-old said, and got up and kissed you.

"Yeah, happy birthday," the thirteen-year-old sleepily muttered from the sofa.

On the table were three gifts wrapped in the leftover glossy red paper and shiny green ribbon from December. A guide to playing better poker, swimming goggles, cuff links.

"Fantastic," you said, kissing everyone. Your wife held out the grocery list to you.

"Do you want to go, or should I?"

"I'll go," you said cheerfully.

"No detours," she said, kissing you, "even if it is your birthday."

"I know." She meant no stopping for the neighborhood pick-me-up, a shot of the local white alcohol with a beer back, served at every bar between your apartment and the supermarket. You hurried to dress and hustled down the stairs and out the door, feeling the remarkable comfort of shorts and a T-shirt after the long week in business suits just passed. On the streets dads strolled with their families, dads in sport coats and polo shirts, dads in cut-off jeans and T-shirts, dads smoking cigarettes and dads avoiding the smokers, dads pushing strollers and dads being pushed along by hormonal teenagers, dads reading the newspaper over their breakfast in a café and dads doting on their pastel-clad kids, dads sitting arm-in-arm with their wives and dads looking off into space, dads full of wonder and dads weighted with indifference or even boredom, dads looking at you and dads looking past you, scores of different dads and none of them us. None of us lived even close to your neighborhood, and most of us rarely visited.

You crossed the broad bustling avenue and entered the cacophony of the supermarket, a voice on the sound system prattling on about ground beef and organic eggs and cheddar cheese and sweet melons and mussels and red wine and white wine and laundry detergent. You moved without having to think with the list in your hand, and your cart seemed to be filling itself as you glided past uniformed women offering samples of mini hot dogs and peanut butter and stuffed pasta and smoked fish. How you loved this supermarket! There were three aisles alone of wine, an entire aisle for ice cream, a large square counter not unlike the bar in your favorite place but this one devoted only to the delicatessen. In your pocket your cell phone vibrated and buzzed.

"I left off marmalade and batteries," she said.

"Got it," you said.

You were headed toward the dairy wing when you saw her, her eyes scanning the packed shelves of nutritional supplements and organic foods. The girls at Girls called her Mammy, and answered *Yes, Mammy* and *No, Mammy* when she rang the room to tell them that time was up and whatever else she might have to say, but you knew her only as the cashier, and never called her Mammy. Your first instinct was to turn your back, shield your face, but she wasn't looking at you, and to glimpse her in the abnormally bright light of the supermarket was such a shock and such a rarity that you just stood there taking her in, the largeness of her girth and the smallness of her face, the innocence of her expression as she searched, and then her arm with its flapping flesh reached up and she pulled down a canister of dried oats and you made yourself move on. You had always wondered what it would be like to see any of them out in the world and Mammy was the closest you had come. You looked back over your shoulder from the safety of the dairy display and she was gone. Mammy. You found yourself moving back toward the organic aisle. You wanted to see her again. Maybe you would introduce yourself and ask how she was doing. You knew you weren't supposed to. She wasn't back in the coffee aisle or the cereal aisle or in any of the three aisles of wine. There were two wings of check-out stiles, and she wasn't in either of them. But you'd seen her. You were sure of it. "Mammy?" you called out above the crowds. "Mammy?" Little children with chocolate on their faces turned to stare at you. Mothers were glaring at you. "Mammy?" What would you say to her? What could you say to her? "Mammy?" You'd left your cart back by the milk. You were going to be late to the park restaurant. You were being ridiculous. Was that her over by the heads of lettuce? "Mammy?" You saw her own head jerk as if hooked by a fisherman, but she made herself not turn. You could feel her wincing. How could you have dared such a thing. "Ma—" You stopped yourself. You made your way meekly back to the milk. You resumed doing what you'd been sent to do. What had you been thinking? What the hell had you been thinking?

We were all ridiculous. Let us not stop short of admitting that. And perhaps we were all unsalvageable.

At home was the usual vanquished chaos, the martyr over the kitchen sink dispatching the last breakfast dish, the children narcotized by the television.

"That took you long enough," she said.

"It was mobbed," you said.

"Get the park bag ready, okay? Just in case."

You put away the groceries and filled the red canvas sack with suntan lotions, flip flops, a frisbee, a mini soccer ball, three bottles of water, a box of crackers, a bottle of ibuprofen and a packet of Band-Aids, the kids' sunglasses, the kids' iPods. The five of you funneled out the door, down the stairs, out onto the street, and into the metro. It was another beautiful day in paradise and the metro smelled of suntan lotion and candy and bubble gum marred by the occasional searing whiff of urine or even excrement. As the connected cars wormed toward the park you could look down the entire length of the train and marvel at the number of axels the whole must have been turning on, four long cars of children, teenagers, men, and women heading toward the park. You all exited at Park Village, and after three escalators and two city blocks found yourselves on the green. Down the ramp, in a corner of restaurants and shops, was the restaurant playfully named Hades. Even though you were ten minutes late, you were the first there.

We arrived in familiar gaggles of toted play supplies, cameras dangling from around our necks, the mâitre d' smiling as we surrendered the better table to our wives and led our children to our situation in the rear of the terrace under an awning and out of view of the gardens. We could still see our spouses, already sipping wine beneath an umbrella around a table that looked out over the greenery and had a view all the way to the horizon. Finally we got soda for the children and several bottles of wine for us, and we could relax. We raised our glasses.

"Happy birthday!"

"Yes, happy birthday!"

"To you!"

"To us!"

"To the kids!"

"To the wives!"

"To the city!"

"Ah, yes, the city!"

There were knowing winks but no references. There were the children, once their food was ordered, breaking off into packs of two or three, the older ones immediately charged with the responsibility of keeping them all in sight and herding them back when the time came. There was a third bottle of wine, then a fourth. Over at their table the wives were having a second. They were too far away for us to hear anything and none of us bothered to speculate. It was your birthday. You were temporarily a hero. We were too far back to see much of the pedestrian traffic, but what we could see was agreeable enough. We liked to look but we'd long lost interest in fantasizing about any pursuit; after all, we knew we preferred paying for it. Why ogle something you couldn't have when you could rent something you wanted?

After lunch, while the children roamed the gardens, our wives beckoned for us to join them. At the table was a wrapped party favor for each of us. We opened them at once, and in our hands were baseball caps with our six or eight names stitched on them as if we all belonged to the same little league team. You pressed yours on, to see if you could feel the innocence, but you felt nothing remarkable. We sat and sipped wine side by side with our increasingly pretty wives. Perhaps it was that the prettier they became, the more disconcerted we all grew, so in retribution they became prettier still. Perhaps it was that.

"So how did you two meet each other?"

For some of us, these were our second spouses, and the question held an intrinsic moral register we did not want to activate. Your wife leapt in. "He was new in our corporation," she said, "in New York, and there was a holiday reception, and I walked in and I saw him slouched near the bar, and he was the only one I recognized from the orientation session I led so I got a scotch and stood by him. Of course," and here she put her arm in yours, "he had nothing good to say about anything. He'd been there only three weeks and he hated his department, the company, the city, everything. I told him, god, why are you telling me all this and why did you even take the job, and he told me it was the only one he'd been offered and even then he'd had to beg for it. I wanted to get up and walk away but I was laughing too hard. 'I have to go take care of a neighbor's pet,' he said, looking at his watch. 'He's an awful dog. You want to come? It should be pretty nasty and involve a lot of fecal matter.' Of course I said no. But can you believe that?"

"Maybe he was showing you," one of us said in the tentative silence that followed the laughter, "how much you could trust him to tell you everything."

"I know," your wife said, smiling, and then the smile fell off her face and her look followed it down into the barely touched dessert on her plate. "But now," she said sadly. She said nothing further.

We rallied then, we had to for you. Each of us dutifully told our stories, stories of office liaisons or blind dates or college romances, each equally familiar and unique, because although we were paradigmatic, we were still ourselves. Your wife dutifully listened with a rapt expression fixed on her tanned pretty face. But all of us noticed the forced gaiety that had crept in and now sat like an unwanted overbearing guest atop our communal table. We could tell you felt you needed to say something, anything, but you sat politely laughing at the appropriate times, trying to wait out the awkwardness that enveloped us all and was this far—*this far*—from splintering into something else entirely, something that might cost all of us a whole hell of a lot of money and who knew what else more. Though some of us had some idea of that, us second-marriage guys. We knew. We ordered champagne to see if that would help, but it might as well have been rock candy, the way we consumed it with a fixed, unnatural, loud determination.

That night you, who never texted, sent a text. We need to talk, you said.

Sleep on it.

When the cell phone rang the next morning, while our wives were off delivering the children to their schools, and your number came up, it was hard to know whether it would be better to answer it or let you have a few more days to navigate things.

"What do you say, captain?"

"I say I can't do this anymore. I say I need to tell her everything." There was a slight panting quality, as if you were out of breath, perhaps from climbing those stairs in your tall narrow row house.

"Then all that there will be left is to hand over the keys."

"It's a weird feeling," you said, sounding like a kid. "I keep looking around this house imagining this is the last time I will get to see it. I keep looking at the suitcase in the closet and knowing I will have to pack it."

"It doesn't have to be that way, you know. You could just stop and become like everyone else. Bury a past that nobody really knows anything about. She only suspects you, captain. She doesn't *know* anything."

"I have to tell her. That lunch yesterday. It was just. I want to blow this up."

"Oh, you'll blow up all right. Can't you hear yourself, captain? It's all I, I, I. What about the rest of us?"

"I know the deal," you said.

"The wives talk. They've been talking for a long time. I hear it came up. We came up, captain. If I have one thing to tell you it is this. There is no I, captain. It's all we."

"I need to do this," you said. "I can't . . . I wasn't . . ."

"You sound like a goddamn girl, captain. I heard one of the wives thinks you have a feminine side."

"We all have feminine sides, you idiot."

"Sure we do, captain. Sure we do. I'll take my feminine side up, with big boobs and her pubic hair shaved in that strip that I like. How about you?"

"I'm going to tell her."

"Sure you are. You keep looking around that place of yours and imagining yourself not in it. Your side of the bed, you're not in it. Your favorite chair in front of the television, you're not in it. Your seat at the dinner table, you're not in it. Your crapper, you're not on it. I bet you love that crapper of yours. And I bet you love the way your kids are in the morning before they open their mouths. And I bet you love your wife in the morning, too. Or late at night when you're lying awake in bed and realizing just how cozy your little world is in our frenetic city. And that's why you're doing this, right, because you love her and you want to make her happy? That makes no fucking sense at all—"

"I'm not doing it for that. I'm doing it to rediscover honesty and legitimacy. I'm doing it for a second chance."

"There are no second chances, you fool. There is one chance, and it is continuous until you stop breathing. Everything you've done will be part of what you do next. There's no escaping it. You can't right a so-called wrong. And let me underscore that I do not think this is wrong. Men like us, we're doing what comes naturally."

"Then tell your wife. If it's goddamn natural, tell her. Let's all tell our wives and just see what comes next."

"For one thing, captain, we won't be able to afford what comes next. For a long time we won't be able to afford anything.

Not a girl at our favorite place, not a drink at our favorite bar, not even our stupid little poker game."

"Why does everything have to be about money?"

"Because it is, captain. It is. And there is nothing wrong about that either. Consider our political system. Consider our way of life. Everything you get, you get with money. There isn't a damn free thing left in this world. You pay for love, you pay for weather, you pay for the bed you sleep in, you pay for your kids, you pay to take a crap, you pay to walk around even when you don't buy anything. There isn't a damn thing we can do that doesn't cost something. It costs us even to talk to each other!"

"It costs us a lot," you said quietly. "It has cost us really quite a lot."

"Very good. You turned it on me. I like that. Listen, captain, it occurs to me that confession can't be the only way out of this problem you are making. Maybe you should at least come to our poker game today and listen to some reasoning before you take this any further?"

"You have got to be kidding me." You were laughing then. "You used to be in the military, for god's sake. You've probably killed a man or two."

"I probably have. I probably have. Certainly I trained some people."

"In the Middle East!" you said.

"That's right, captain. Damn you got a good memory."

"I remember everything," you said. You were not making a threat, which was appreciated. "I'm not afraid of you. Or of course I'm afraid of you, but that's really not the point. The point is I'm done with poker. I'm done with the whole scene."

"I'm glad to know that about the fear, captain. I really am. You have nothing to be afraid of from me. You and I, we're like brothers. I was there for your first time. You thanked me."

"I remember," you said, without bitterness or irony. "I was very grateful. Look, I can do this without involving anyone else."

"Sure you can, captain. Sure you can."

"So have you?" you said.

"Have I what?"

"Have you killed a man?"

"You know, what with the weapons technology, with the range and whatnot, I really couldn't say."

"The range," you repeated, thinking about that, considering it. "The range."

"And devices that are time-delay. Who knows with those things? You're not even there to see it. I've never seen any of my own, captain, so like I said, I really couldn't say. Seriously, though, you need to lighten up."

"Did you see her face? Everyone saw her face."

"Then you saw her face, so you must be a believer?"

"Shut up—"

"Do you have any doubts in your mind?"

"I mean it!"

"Are you in love . . . vvvvvvvvvvvv."

"I'm hanging up."

"You're a believer, so you couldn't leave her if you dared."

You hung up.

It was easy to shut one's eyes and see the world as we knew it forever changed, the move out to the apartment of shame, the descent into the alimony graveyard, where all fine bank accounts went to die. The secret lives of men were rarely pretty, and when they were exposed they were instantly assigned an unpleasant odor, because that was what moral condemnation was all about. To hold one's nose, turn up one's nose, look down one's nose. What we would give for a whole city of broken noses. Instead there was the split scene, as the teenagers called it, where fathers of certain kids they knew had been exiled and the children ended up discovering the advantages of two sets of accommodation, two sets of lives; these were the men who had been caught, the men who'd had affairs. They were men we did not know and they were men we weren't going to get to know. One was a chemist at a multinational drug firm, another owned a car rental company, a third had a glass factory in a northern suburb. Their names were Bob, Steve, Joseph. We'd never met them, but we'd certainly heard of them. The rumor was that they were not good men, but who knew? We'd met the wives; the wives were invited everywhere. They were alternately sullen or sultry, moody or mischievous, determined or downtrodden. You could not predict how they'd be from moment to moment, mostly you just wanted to stay out of their way, especially if you were us, convinced that they had a particular antenna for anything we might have been up to. Perhaps, even, they wouldn't mind a little scheme or indulgence of entrapment. Misery wanted company. We already had all the company we wanted.

At poker it was just us five or seven, quitting work at three as we sometimes tried to do. It was a game now none of us wanted to play and yet we had to keep ourselves from hurrying to finish.

"We could kill him," someone said, and it was hard to tell whether it was a joke or a surrender to the fact that this would never come to pass.

"We could."

"Oh, come on."

"What if he talks?"

"He isn't going to talk. What would he say?"

"We should never have included him."

"Don't be a fool. He's the one who brought us together."

"That's why you always called him captain."

"He always did have a plan."

"I think I might head back to work."

"Don't be absurd."

Outside the bar, above Christ's Church, the sun was squinting at us. Across the street a waiter pulled down the grate over a restaurant's glass storefront. Up ahead, on a small square by a stilled fountain, two withered women in wheelchairs were weakly tossing breadcrumbs at gleeful pigeons while their attendants chattered on in a language we were sure not to recognize.

"Well?"

"I think we should go on to the soccer games, to keep on top of things."

"I told you he wouldn't be able to handle it."

"Could you guys just be quiet already?"

In the cars we were quiet, listening for inspiration. Our stunted caravan circumnavigated the square and soon we were headed out of town. To our left, some miles away, the water glistened in its late spring sheen, and you could almost see the tiny dots of people's heads bobbing in it. We pulled off the highway, parked near the fields, pried ourselves from the cars, slouched through the open gate onto the green expanse of the eight or so fields.

"Well, if it isn't the dreamers," one of our wives said. "What are you boys doing here?"

"We were curious. We haven't been to a game in a long time."

"They're just ending," another wife said wryly, the one who wore the tightest jeans and clearly thought she was hot. They were all ever hotter, and other people would want them. Other people could really want them. And sometimes these days when we wanted them they more and more didn't want us, as if they did know something, or as if they liked us even less or they liked sex even less, or both, and who could blame them? "Have too much to drink at poker?"

The head of the league crossed the field toward us. "Ladies and gentlemen," he said. He smiled at us from within the artfully cultivated scruff of his facial hair. Would he just end up a footnote to a super-embarrassing soccer-father scandal, or would he be free to continue his usual pattern of staccato bursts of futile fund-raising interrupted by long periods of thoughtfully staring across the green expanse? Past our little throng he glimpsed the arrival of someone even wealthier than we were. "Will you excuse me?" he said.

We all turned to watch the approach, the handshake, the shared solemn grin as if there were no business more serious than our children's sports lives. Wasn't he the guy who'd had to fire a coach of the twelve-year-olds for doing the assistant coach in the gym supply room while the kids were dutifully executing dribbling skills outside?

"I had a dream about him," a wife said. "I dreamed he actually did something."

We turned upon each other in roaring laughter. What did everyone know? What did anyone know?

"Hey, where's the captain?"

We all looked around as if expecting to find you among us.

"And his lovely bride?" one of us said.

The whistle blew and those of us with younger children went off to hunt for them in the gym, while others stood animatedly and waited for their children to find them. Usually we would hang back while the women engaged in the pursuit, but we were now newly devoted husbands and many of us slyly draped arms around our wives' waists or shoulders and strolled off, as if it took two to fetch one child. We had been around a long time, and we all knew that never was hypocrisy bolder than when it was on the brink of being exposed or betrayed or both. We cast glances at one another, assessing ourselves for the proper posture of dutiful affection. This was who we might have to be for a long time to come, and we wanted to get it right so we would no longer have to think about it. On our way into the vibrating gymnasium we glimpsed each other's nods of approval.

Within too bright walls decorated with pieces of their latest artwork, our U-8s and U-6s waited, and we plucked them from the crowds of curious and overeager and indomitable parents and the cluster of exhausted but relieved coaches and assistant coaches. There was your boy, his blue-gray knapsack already on his back, a bright green craft project of glued popsicle sticks clutched in his hand, eyeing us expectantly. We hustled our own families from the gym.

In the mobbed but already emptying parking lot your older daughter stood with your younger daughter, her hand gripping her cell phone. "I tell you," she was saying, "I tried and tried and they're not answering."

"Maybe they left them at home," your younger daughter said.

"What's up, girls?" one of us had to ask, as the wives looked on.

"I'll go get him," your older daughter said, ignoring us. "You stay here. Don't move."

"Okay," your younger daughter grumbled.

"Is everything okay?"

Your older daughter took us in as if for the first time. "They're just late, is all. I'll be right back."

We watched her stride across the fields and disappear inside the gymnasium.

"I hope they're not having too much fun without us," one of the wives said.

"You ladies are relentless."

"You have no idea where your parents are?"

"Nope," the younger girl said, looking at the ground, kicking an invisible stone. "No idea."

Our own crowd had dwindled, pulled away by impatient or hungry or thirsty kids or the myriad of further after-school activities that plagued them. There was a silence as we remaining pairs all looked brightly at each other, eyebrows arching above sunglasses in unphrased questions, mouths frozen in smiles that were intended to soothe any doubt. Our own children raced around shrieking, momentarily free in a vast expanse where they were almost always under rein. Your older daughter stepped across the parking lot, holding her little brother by the hand so tightly that his green project seemed in danger of snapping.

"No sign?" she called across.

"No sign," her sister muttered.

She came right up to us. Her face was filled with innocence and worry and annoyance and a flicker of fear.

"Let me give you my cell number," one of the wives said. "Do you have enough money?" The three wives reached into their purses at once, as if money could solve anything. It was true; they could just take a cab.

Your older daughter wouldn't hear of it. "The bus is much better," she said.

We all knew your family was watching their money. We were all watching our money. We were watching it go out the window. Though it was true that unlike you we could afford it, it was still not that much fun to watch.

Your children started off down the hill.

"Go with them," a wife murmured.

"What?"

"They can't fit in our cars, so one of you will have to go with them."

"She can handle it."

"She's never done it before. Go with them and make us all happy."

"All the way?"

"All the way." All the wives nodded at that.

"I'll go."

"I'll go."

"I really can't."

Two was better than one, and besides, if we played it right, we could wring an extra half hour out of it.

"We'll go." We slouched off after the kids. "We'll be home by dinner."

"Surely before then!" one of them called after us. "And be nice to the kids. They might need a snack or a drink."

We waved good-bye without looking back. Below, beyond the fields, the kids turned right. We picked up our pace to keep them in sight.

"You think it's better to hang back and give them their space?"

"Seeing as this is an official assignment and we will be held responsible, no."

"Do you think anything awful has happened?"

"It's doubtful but still possible."

"Oh god."

"It'll be all right. And if not, then this will be the first true test of all our friendship, and then we'll see where we really stand."

"I hate it when you talk like that."

"Me too."

When we caught up to them your daughter turned and glanced at us as if she'd been expecting us and dreading us at the same time. "Hey," she said.

Your five-year-old began chopping the air and kicking out his feet. "On guard," he said. "Cowabunga!"

Your thirteen-year-old kept looking at the ground. Your older daughter held your hyperactive son from us and looked at us unblinkingly.

"We . . . uh . . . we have some business in your neighborhood, so we just thought we'd tag along in case we could be of any use."

"Sure," she said. "Sounds good."

"It was our wives' idea."

"It's really fine." She looked both ways and pulled her brother across the street. The younger daughter walked like an actress at the end of a movie, staring far off toward the blurred horizon as if waiting for the credits to roll. At the bus stop—a bus, we hadn't been on a bus since our teens!—the kids sat in an orderly row on the one bench and we leaned like guards to either side. There was a soda machine and a candy machine.

"Can we get you guys anything?"

"They're broken," your older daughter said. She shook her head as if in disbelief at all the money those machines must have eaten before that was figured out. "So what were you guys up to today?"

"We played poker at a new place on the square not far from here. Too much beer and too many peanuts, though. I think some of us had trouble getting out of our chairs."

"Wasn't my dad supposed to be there?"

"He said he was done with poker for a while. I think he just wants to lose a little weight."

"He does obsess about his weight." She stared down the

hill toward the off-ramp, obviously hoping to see a bus headed our way. "They both do."

"Your mother's perfect."

There was an instant awkward silence.

"All our wives really keep themselves in shape."

She looked from one to the other of us as if she wasn't sure she'd heard that right. "Uh-huh."

We looked at our watches.

"Sometimes," your younger daughter said, "there won't be a bus for half an hour and then there will be two buses. It's pretty annoying."

"So how was school today?"

"Pretty good," your older daughter said, checking her cell phone again.

"The usual," your younger daughter said.

"Shut up, you old bean bag!" your five-year-old shrieked.

"Just try to be polite," your oldest said to him. "I know you don't know what the word means, but just try to be, okay?" She looked accusingly at her cell phone again.

"I am not polite! I am never polite!"

"Where *is* the bus?" your younger daughter said, clutching her head. "God, I have such a headache."

Your oldest rushed over and snared your younger daughter's lunch bag, unzipped it and pulled out a half-full bottle of water. She nudged her sister with it. "Drink it."

"Fine," the younger girl growled.

"She gets dehydrated, and apparently her contact lens prescription is off," the older girl explained. "And then there is the fact of our little brother."

"Oh, he isn't so bad."

"I am VERY BAD," the little boy said. He kicked out his legs and bared his teeth.

"You're only five. How bad can you be?"

"Don't ask him that," your older daughter said.

"This is the longest wait in the history of waits," your younger daughter said.

"We could walk to the next stop," one of us timidly suggested. "Maybe the machines work there, and it's not a bad path beside the highway."

"He won't." Your older daughter nodded at the little boy.

"I sure won't!"

"Don't you think it's odd we haven't heard from them?" your younger daughter said. "I mean, it's been more than thirty minutes since they should have been here."

"Maybe their bus broke down. Or maybe they lost their cell phones."

"Both of them?" Your older daughter examined us closely. "Hey, do you know something? What do you know?"

The bus, thank god, appeared over the crest of the off-ramp.

"Oh, look, there's the bus!" one of us said.

"What *do you know*?" your daughter asked again.

"We don't know anything, kid. And we don't even know what we don't even know."

Your younger daughter giggled at that. The little one jumped up and down. "The bus! The bus!" He seemed to be one of those kids who would talk in exclamation points until he became comatose.

"You know something," your sixteen-year-old said quietly, as she pulled your little boy up onto the bus, both their knapsacks unhinging from their shoulders and threatening to fall onto the curb, and we reached instinctively and steadied them. "I don't know what it is, but that is what I know."

We sat in three rows in the rear of the bus. The driver stepped off and lit a cigarette.

"He gets a break," your younger daughter said. "It's the end of the line and he always gets a break, even if he's thirty minutes late."

"Even if he's a hundred minutes late!" your little boy said.

We started whistling to ourselves and examining our fingernails and feeling our pockets to make sure our phones were still on.

"This is a rare form of torture," your older daughter said.

"Even the view sucks," your younger daughter said. "That's hard to do in this city. My dad says there's a view from everywhere."

"It doesn't suck. It doesn't suck," one of us said, standing up and pointing over the kids through the window. "There's the Water Tower and City Hall and a tiny bit of the port where the ferries push off for the islands. If you look closely I think you can see a few ship masts, even if you can't see the waterfront. And, look, there are people swimming!"

The driver got back on and started the bus.

"Thank god," your older daughter said.

We fell quiet as the bus bopped up onto the highway.

"Go, go!" the little boy said.

"It takes about seventy-five minutes," your younger daughter explained. "Or eighty."

"Of course it does."

If was hard to believe it was still only Monday. It was hard to believe the damn town was so big, and if your place was any farther from the soccer fields it would have been in the water. It was hard to believe we had to be doing this for you. As we re-entered the city, the bus lumbered along like some overweight and old water buffalo, pausing at every demarcated stop as if expecting to find sustenance. We looked at each other and made a silent pact not to check our watches. Your children read books and thumb-wrestled and bit their nails and looked out the window whenever there was anything to look at, lemon trees and tiger lilies, a bent-over construction guy showing his butt crack, that long avenue of fashion stores and gourmet shops, a line of policemen contending with a small union protest, gypsies selling jewelry made of tin, packed bar after packed bar, the sidewalks populated by an overflow of giddy smokers and drinkers. The town was like a rose, an oasis, a maze, a minefield, a string of possible metaphors for itself that went on beyond forever.

By the time we got to your stop your five-year-old was asleep, his little face creased and puckered.

"Can you carry him?" your daughter asked.

We took turns carrying him. He was a heavier kid than he looked, and the blocks fell away very slowly, the streets crowded with late-afternoon shoppers and hawkers and pickpockets and gawkers and buskers. There were bands playing at the first three or four corners, and the usual horde in front of the loudest bar, and getting through the mobs was no picnic, and all the time we felt we ought to be clinging to our wallets, and the closer we came to your apartment the more we worried about what was going on up there. It was now more than ninety minutes since one of you should have showed up at soccer, and the unmentioned, of course, was that there'd been no sign of anything unusual along the bus route, no sign at all. Your daughters were holding hands that last block down the narrow, charming street where not even cars could squeeze, and in the shadows of the buildings the afternoon seemed suddenly to give way to night even though there were three hours left of sun in the sky. At your row house's door your older daughter took the little boy back onto her shoulder, gave him a hug and a swing of her shoulders, and set him on his feet on the pavement.

"We're home, honey," she said as the boy rubbed his eyes. She smiled at the both of us. "We'll be okay now. Look," she waved something shiny, "I've got a key and everything."

"You sure it's all right?"

"I do this all the time by myself. Now I've got my sister and brother. We're fine."

"Okay." We started off down the street.

"And thank you!" she called out.

We waved as if it were no big deal. As we rounded the corner and saw the kids entering your home, we made ourselves keep walking. It was really the only thing to do.

Check all that apply:

I have already experienced a rush to judgment, outrage, and condemnation.

I have discerned elements of true moral ambiguity.

I can no longer look at myself in the mirror.

I understand that society is vast and complex, and while I cannot condone the sexual misbehavior of others, I am not in a position to condemn it.

I expect there will eventually be violence, as that comes with this kind of territory.

Telling the complete truth can be a bad strategy.

Truth is not a strategy, it is the right of each partner in any union.

Never admit anything, because then all that is left is to surrender the keys.

Think of the children.

If you have children, a higher moral standard applies.

Having children can actually lower the moral standards one must meet; this depends on a lot of factors.

The only worthwhile purpose of life is the practice of truth and art.

Pleasure must have some role, but at what cost?

Where is religion?

I have never contemplated anything aberrant.

Aberrant behavior is what makes us human.

People who employ the "human" excuse are actually animals.

Almost everything that happens is only natural.

You do indeed always pay for it.

I have *never* paid for it in my life.

I am in denial.

We stopped at that bar at the mouth of the metro station where we'd often met before our expeditions. It was still as bright as day, women proudly carrying oversized name shopping bags delicately containing their small but expensive purchases, tourists sipping beer with their fat elbows up on the little round tables, a mime entertaining a loud thicket of people who seemed to have no idea they were being set up to have their wallets and purses lifted.

"Another day in paradise."

"Do you think we should go back?"

"I'm a forward thinker. I never go back."

The waiter came.

"Two locals, please."

We checked our watches.

"There's no time for the other thing."

"You want a cigarette?"

"No, I don't want a cigarette. You want a cigarette?"

Neither of us smoked, though occasionally one of us would carry a pack reserved for you. That was how highly we thought of you. The shots of white alcohol and the beer backs came. They filled our little table.

"To?"

"To never going back."

"To never going back, then, except to the Pink Pearl."

"How many are we up to now?"

"I have no idea. Wasn't he the one who was keeping track?"

"You ever been to that place around the corner from where we watched the Super Bowl?"

"Seventy-six? Where they bring all the girls in at once and you have to choose yours in front of all the others? Sure, I went with him."

"So did I. That was a good place."

"Clean and new. I had this Colombian who wouldn't let me stop, even when the condom broke. She was wild. He was sad after that place, too."

"He was?"

"He took the blonde, as everywhere. She told him she'd been there only ten days. They did a lot of kissy face. When he turned her on her belly and did it that way she clenched her fists as if she were really doing something, as if she were really feeling something, and for some reason it reminded him of when he used to put his kids down for their naps and they'd clench their little fists. Weird guy."

"Sensitive."

"So what do you think is going on?"

"I wouldn't want to speculate. Nothing good, I bet."

"Are we betting? I bet nothing happened. I bet he got some fear and intelligence and kept his goddamn mouth shut. I bet he got religion. That's what I bet."

"You are a wishful bettor."

"I've been around."

"We've all been around."

"So what do you think our wives have been up to?"

"Our wives? They're definitely getting hotter, but I haven't a clue. When I get one, then someone will pay, and it won't be me."

"You really don't have any idea?"

"I've done everything short of sticking a Minicam in her what-what, and I've got nothing."

The check came without our asking. That was another thing about us. All the waiters everywhere always seemed to know we'd be moving on.

"You want to go back down and have a look? I think we should have a look."

"You're an aggressive guy."

"I'm in advertising, for god's sake."

"If it's bad, I don't think we want to be there."

"It's not bad." We rose. "Come on, don't be a chicken shit. *I'm* going."

"You're really going?"

"Sure, it's in my blood. Besides, it's the only way I'm gonna get any sleep tonight. *Did you see them,* my wife will ask. *What was their excuse?*"

"That's not the only reason."

"'Course not. Besides, he's got to have another bottle of something to pour for us."

We slouched back to your row house and rang the bell. No answer.

"That's weird."

"Maybe they went out for dinner."

"On a school night? They have a rule that they don't do *anything* on a school night."

"Maybe it's a special occasion."

There was no visible light in the windows and none coming from under the door.

"Either out or asleep."

"Or they're all dead inside."

We turned to go. Voices—people—were coming around

the corner. We shrugged at each other. The first we saw was your older daughter's hair. She looked at us in surprise.

"Oh, hey."

"We thought your dad himself should give us a drink for bringing you home," we explained.

"Yes, of course. But they're still not home and I still haven't heard from them," she tried to say matter-of-factly as we moved aside and gave them space on the landing.

"Oh," one of us said. "Is that unusual?"

"Kind of." She briskly opened the door to the dark row house. Each of them was carrying a white plastic bag of take-out food. "It's unheard of," she said in an almost inaudible voice.

The younger kids raced in and promptly ran up the stairs. Your daughter hustled after them, gaining the kitchen, pulling out plates and silverware. You could see she was just trying to keep everything as normal as possible. She was doing pretty well for a sixteen-year-old. We stood in the upstairs doorway silently deciding our course. When she turned around she had to adjust what appeared to be a stricken expression.

"Do you need money or anything?"

She shook her head.

"Do you need us to go or stay?"

She shook her head again. "Whatever you're doing, could you maybe go back downstairs and shut the door to the street, please? I can hear that it's open."

"Fine idea."

We shut the door and went back upstairs and again stood in the kitchen doorway watching them; then our cell phones went off all at once and all of us reached for them, even your daughter for hers, though hers hadn't rung and she probably knew it. She instantly slid hers back into the pocket of her soccer shorts as if she were ashamed of it.

"Yeah, I'm still here."

"Yeah, we're with the kids. No word yet."

We listened to our wives instructing and speculating.

"Okay."

"Sure."

We hung up and smiled apologetically at your daughter. From twenty feet away the Disney Channel was blasting at us. Your two younger children sat close together on the pumpkin sofa. This was getting a little difficult.

"Is there anyone you can call?"

"Just you guys." She tried to laugh and it came out like a girlish squeak. "And you're already here."

"So we can check that off the list. Look, we're going to hang out and just play it by ear. It's not like our wives would let us come home at this point anyway."

"Okay." She nodded gratefully, but we didn't want to embarrass her by noticing.

"So, kids. Dinner on the couch in front of the television. How good is that?"

The little one squawked with delight and raised his hands over his head like he'd just won a prize fight.

"Whatever," mumbled your younger daughter.

It was weird to be behind the door and inside your life. You had a nicer place than you thought. The big still-life painting, the deep green wall, the domesticated palm tree, the built-in entertainment center. Sure it was tight, sure it could have used a view, sure we never could have lived there ourselves, but it was a pretty nice place for what it was, and the location, it was hard to beat the location, if that was the location you wanted. The densest neighborhood in the city, the place where it all happened, all those bars and restaurants within walking distance, every kind of store, even the art museum was sort of across the street. Never a problem to get a cab. It was a good life you were apparently in the process of blowing to shreds.

We helped get the kids served and made sure your older daughter sat down in front of her food, and then we poured ourselves drinks and sat, with the oppressive television still going. It was hard to think but it would have been harder to make conversation. Your older daughter kept looking at us when she thought we weren't looking at her. We all tried to interest ourselves in the show. It was a teen sit-com about kids at the beach or kids in a rock band or both. It had a perky Asian girl in it who we liked a lot, and for some reason that particular episode featured a beach volleyball tournament, and we had enough to look at.

"They have homework," your older daughter said.

"What?" we both said.

"The kids have homework and it's getting late."

We checked our watches. Now it was past seven thirty and hurtling ominously toward eight. For a slow day things were going extremely fast.

"Kids, is this show almost over?"

"Sure."

"Yeah."

"After this there will be homework, okay?" one of us said. "And then what, baths?"

"Today is not the day," your older daughter said.

"When is the day?"

"Hopefully a day when we won't be here, idiot," we interrupted each other before she could answer.

"Oh, right. Right."

"Every family's got its own routine, you know."

"I know. I just got ahead of myself, is all."

"When do we call the police?" your older daughter asked almost in a whisper.

"Oh, I don't think it's going to come to that. Any minute they'll come walking through that door and there will be a logical explanation for everything."

"Okay," your daughter said. "Would you guys even say what you really thought?"

"Not if we can help it."

"The truth is overrated. The truth is never a good idea. Pick one."

Even though we had our backs to the show, we kept looking at it; talking through the soundtrack was like chewing ice. All the kids on the show seemed to have the exact same damn voice, and that too was distracting, though being distracted was not a bad thing. It kept us from getting too involved or thinking we were involved in the first place. Who knew what would have been said or done if that TV was off. Maybe that was why it was there. The credits began to roll and your daughter snapped it off with the remote. The younger children, two intertwined and nearly indistinguishable lumps on the sofa, moaned.

"So, kids, homework?"

Without warning your younger daughter started crying, big tears, lots of them, streaming down her face, her shoulders shuddering, heaving. She was sobbing, and the TV was off, and we could hear every gasp and gulp. Her little brother tapped her or patted her. "It's okay," he said.

"What do you want me to do?" your older daughter asked.

"I want Mom," your younger daughter sobbed. "I want Mommy."

We rose gently from our chairs.

"How about some ice cream? There must be some ice cream or some cookies."

"Nooo," she wailed, furiously shaking her head.

"Do you want to take a walk? Get some fresh air?"

"WHY ARE YOU EVEN HERE?" she screamed at us.

We looked at each other. We turned to your older daughter as the wailing rose and crashed around us.

"We could. We could just hang out downstairs by the door, and, you know, when you need us you could just buzz us in? Maybe that's the thing to do?"

Your older daughter nodded as she hugged her sister. Her own face was red, too, mottled with the burden of everything. Your little boy seemed to be holding on to them both. He was smiling. Maybe he thought it was some kind of game to get rid of the old guys. We filled our glasses—perhaps a sign we weren't going anywhere—and let ourselves out. We shut the door softly, softly stepped down the stairs in case there was anything to hear. On the street, true to our word, we waited by the door.

"Well, that was intense."

"I had no idea teenagers even cried."

"How long have they been AWOL?"

We both knew the answer to that.

"Not so long."

"No, I guess not."

"It could be a lot worse."

"It might be."

At the same time we each took out our pack of cigarettes reserved for you and lit one apiece and started to smoke.

"If there ever was a time."

"Exactly."

We squinted up and down the street. At least it wasn't getting dark yet.

"How many weeks left of school?"

"Ten days, man."

"Your kids going to the soccer camp?"

"I don't know what the plan is."

"My kid is."

"Probably mine are, too, then."

"When do you travel?"

"All the time. Every week I gotta be somewhere."

"Gonna order takeout?"

"We'll see."

We both laughed.

"We're incorrigible."

"We'll never learn."

"Or we've learned what there is to learn, and this is why we've become what we are."

"Sure."

"Exactly."

"What do you think is going to happen here?"

"I have no idea."

"On the way over to soccer one of the guys was saying that the last time someone got caught—years ago, another city, but the same deal of guys getting busy together—it was an e-mail thing and he took the hit alone. Lost the keys, moved to a rental, the whole deal."

"You have to be really careful on e-mail."

"Let me ask you this. If your wife came to you and just outright said she was paying men to have sex with her, what would you do?"

"Hell, I don't know. I'd probably kill her."

"That's why this honesty thing sucks."

"Exactly."

"So he saw his wife's face fall into her uneaten dessert and that was it?"

"I guess so."

"There's nothing like things getting a little real."

"I think this might be the longest day of my life in a long time."

"Imagine how he feels."

We stood there smoking our cigarettes trying to imagine how you felt. There was something about what happened when a man set out to bring down the world around him and succeeded that could be truly revelatory, in terms of the human condition, but we hadn't gotten there yet. Remember when you were told that surely we were all great friends but the real test would be when we hit a rough patch? We all knew a patch was going to come, a code somewhere would be broken. We just hadn't foreseen this . . . this confessional type of occurrence, if you will. We didn't believe in confession. We feared being caught, but confession was not on the table. You put it there, you made it happen, and now all hell was breaking loose in your row house. This was why people really didn't want to know. This was why confession was never a play. Bring all that hell down on you like that? That's not logical, it's not advisable, it certainly isn't warranted. Didn't we tell you never to admit anything? You knew how it was supposed to go: *I don't know, I wasn't there. If I was there, I didn't do it. If I did it, it wasn't my fault.* And that was only when confronted by incontrovertible evidence, like if she walked in in the middle. Why the hell did you think every single one of these places had someone just to let you in the door? They weren't supermarkets, for god's sake, they weren't Bloomingdale's or Sears out in the damn suburbs. And none of us used credit cards or were dumb enough to proposition anyone on the street. We had ourselves all covered until you gave in to what you thought you saw it was doing to your wife. You didn't even know what you were looking at! And on top of that, none of us really knew what was going on with our wives!

"We should have killed him."

"Maybe."

We both laughed.

"Hell, you say that, but *I've* never killed anybody."

"I don't even know what I've done. For all I know I might be as pure as the driven snow."

"I bet you say that to all the girls."

"You kidding me? That line never works."

"Then how do you know?"

We laughed again, flimsy laughs. We were headed into some serious weather and it was long past time to think of possible gear or shelter or evac routes. We crushed our cigarettes out and stood there with our hands jammed in our pockets like a couple of virgin school boys who didn't even know what a woman was like and whose immediate future held more of the same.

"It's a great town."

"Sure it's a great town."

"But that won't make anything easier."

"Exactly."

"We'll figure something out."

"We always do."

"It's only the waiting that drives me nuts. I don't like to wait on anything. That's why I had to come down here. I like to know as soon as there is anything to know."

"Waiting can be good. Number one, nothing definitive has happened yet. Number two, one can strategize, *anticipate*."

"That's not the way we think in advertising. In advertising, we do. We don't wait for anything. I remember once—"

"No war stories, please."

We looked at each other oddly, the slightest frisson in the air.

"We don't know each other well, do we?"

"No, we sure don't."

We stood there chewing on that, like we were chewing on something we didn't want to swallow but couldn't spit out.

"Man, for a street in the artists' quarter, there isn't much action."

"That's for damn sure."

It was as calm as a little town on that street. At either end we could see the hustle and the bustle, the flim and the flam, the back and forth, but nobody came up or down your little street.

"It's beginning to get dark."

"I guess so."

"Hell, it *is* dark."

"It got dark a long time ago."

"What did your wife say?"

"To stay as long as it takes."

"Mine, too." We took out fresh cigarettes. "You bring a change of clothes?"

"I brought what was on my mind."

"You and your Zen military shit."

"You and your douchebag advertising shit."

"So what's the strategy?"

"It will come. It always comes at the right time and it hasn't come yet so it must not be the right time."

Now it was pretty dark. The lonely Mexican restaurant down the street had its storefront display lights on, and a waiter came out and lit a cigarette and nodded all the way up the street at us as if he could tell we were the only punks out.

"You don't think the kid thinks we left her, do you?"

Reluctantly we checked our watches, smoke curling momentarily around our wrists, our drinks long empty.

"The thing is, if we rang, we might wake somebody."

"You'd think a mother would be desperate to get back to her children, that that would be her first move."

"I think shock and humiliation would be her first move, and then I don't know."

"What would your wife do if you confessed to her?"

"First, that would never happen. I'd sooner shoot myself than confess, and both would have the same outcome, because we're both a very good shot. So, second, the better question is what would happen if my wife found out everything or, say, most of the things I've been into. Incontrovertible and all that, and she herself was totally innocent. I have some defenses up for that scenario, some safety nets, probably nothing I'm prepared to share right now. What about your wife?"

"What about my wife?"

"If you confessed or whatever."

"She probably wouldn't care. She'd probably find some of it amusing, some not. She'd probably say something like *Let me know when you get it out of your system* or *Just get it out of your system*."

"That's a good wife."

"I've got a good wife."

"We've all got good wives, give or take some issues. But you aren't telling your wife anytime soon because . . . ?"

"Because I don't need to. But I really don't think there'd be a huge problem."

"Sure."

"Nobody really knows anybody else's wife."

"At least not in our little group."

We peered up at your second-story window. The light was still on, the curtains drawn, the shutters still open. That was about all we could see from the distance and the angle.

"I think his wife is kind of hot."

"You've mentioned that before."

"I wonder why they don't do it more often."

"I believe he said something along the lines that when she was pregnant with their fourth she was so pissed at him she wouldn't go near him, and for the year after her miscarriage he was so pissed at her having been so pissed at him that he reciprocated."

"And once they both fell off that horse it was hard to get back on?"

"Something like that."

"What a waste."

"The girls don't help, of course. Once you're getting girls in their early twenties, it's hard to go back to the woman in her mid-forties. He always said that."

"He did. He did."

We finished our cigarettes and crushed them out and looked blankly but searchingly at each other.

"I guess it's out of the question to dash off for a quick drink?"

"Out of the question. They're just kids up there, you know, alone for the moment in the big city. For all we know they could be orphans. Besides, our wives would kill us."

"Why does it always have to be about death with you?"

"It's a motivational tool. In the military they don't train you to shoot to wound."

"Great. Give me a second, will you?"

He loped down the street and turned into the Mexican restaurant. It was easy to ascertain his mission. Soon he came back with a pitcher of margaritas, two glasses, and an order in for a deluxe nacho platter with everything.

"It struck me that we never ate."

"That's true; we didn't."

"I'm thinking if it hits midnight we ring the buzzer gently just once and see if we get an answer."

"I can agree to that."

We stood there drinking. There was no place to sit. These artists' quarter streets might be all the rage but people of our age and class did not sit in them.

"There's only one thing more we need."

"Hah."

"It's important to stick with the thing that got us into this fix in the first place."

"I couldn't agree more."

"Why do men love their dicks so much?"

"That is the eternal question."

"That, and what's the next new place to get some."

"We're going to need another pitcher soon."

"We need it now."

"Of course. But we still have about a third and we must stay sober."

"You can be one proper dude. To the military!"

We toasted the military.

"You think all this will get edited out?"

"It might be. We'll have to see. How many nondisclosure agreements do you think we'll get back anyway?"

"Ten? Still, I hope this all stays. I hope people get a good long look at us and understand that sexual depravity in this kind of way is just fucking normal. People don't need to kill each other over stuff like this. People don't need to get fired and vilified and strung up in the media over consensual sex with people who aren't their spouses. Why does it always have to go down like that? Every week there's some story about somebody. I just don't get it. Or, I get it but it shouldn't be this way. If some good-looking chick wants to make a living on her back and I want to pay for some of that, that ought to be fine. End of story."

"All this from a guy whose wife wouldn't mind?"

"Well, god, they all mind. Everybody minds. They just each express it differently." He sighed and gulped the last of his margarita. "I know, I know. You can't defend us. You can't justify us. We're just despicable. And now probably one of us is dead or something." He handed the glass over. "I'll get us another pitcher and see what the hell happened to our nachos." He stomped off up the street. The cell rang and there was no choice but to answer it.

"So, what's the story?" she wanted to know.

"The story is stopped, is the story. The story is status quo. The story is we're standing out on their little street because the kids basically asked us to leave. The story is that nobody knows what the story is. What the hell is your story? And I want the truth, damn it."

"Have you been drinking?"

"Of course I've been drinking. Why ask something you already know?"

"Listen, you can't get drunk."

"That's what I was just telling—"

"I mean, you really can't. Who knows what's going on and eventually you might need to—"

"I know. I know."

"I'm glad you're there, though. We're all fine here."

"I'm glad. And of course I'm glad you're glad."

"This is all so odd. And you really don't know anything about it?"

"I don't."

"Aren't you the one closest to him?"

"I thought I was."

"The girls were just saying—obviously we've been talking—that maybe in a while we ought to call her father or something."

"That old fart? He lives all the way across the country, and he never wants to deal with the kids on his own. I know that for a fact."

"Or maybe his mother. Or her sister. Four hours is a lot—"

"Four hours is four hours. We've still got time, and there's no reason to go all premature."

The nachos arrived with the pitcher of margaritas and we exchanged knowing looks with each other.

"Did you not hear what I was saying?" the wife said.

"Were you talking? I'm sorry. Look, some nachos have just arrived and we're going to have a little something to eat. Let me get back to you with an update in about an hour. Okay?"

"Okay."

"Okay."

We sat in the street eating the nachos and drinking the margaritas. God knows we were tired. The truth was we were getting a little angry with you. The truth was we were all talked out. The truth was if we saw you walking down the street right now we might have sliced you up right there. We were that pissed.

"Son of a bitch."

"Exactly."

"When was the last time you did something like this?"

"You mean sit in a crappy street in a pair of pants that cost me three hundred? I'd have to say never."

"As soon as I'm done I'm ringing the bell."

"You are?"

"It's been a goddamn hour. That's like seven hours in dog years. That's long enough."

"Okay."

"I was sure you were going to resist."

"I have to take a leak."

"That? That you could do right here. In fact probably right where you're sitting."

We both stood up.

"This is ridiculous."

"Outrageous."

He hit the bell briefly, expertly. He hit the bell like all he ever did was hit bells like that, with absolute minimum impact. We looked down and were surprised to see the second empty pitcher.

"I could piss in that."

"We must be drunk."

"Either that or very old."

"Hello?" Her voice on the intercom sounded fuzzy, muffled, as if she'd been sleeping.

"Remember us?"

"Oh. Sorry. I forgot."

"Everything okay up there?"

"Yeah. I think. Everyone's asleep. What time is it?"

"Nine thirty. Can we come up and use your facilities?"

"My what? Oh, sure. Let me just. Give me a few minutes, okay?" She clicked off before we could answer.

When we looked up the street *you* were standing there.

"Is she up there?" you said.

"Who?" We were stumbling in the street trying to decide whether we should hug you or beat the crap out of you.

"My wife," you said. "Is she up there?"

We shook our heads. "What happened to you? You look awful."

"It was awful," you said. "You were right. I never should have. I never should have become who I am."

"You told her everything?"

"Everything. About me, I told her everything."

"Jesus."

"What an idiot."

"Yet he's still alive."

You started for the door. "Are the kids all right? You've been watching out for them? That was incredible of you guys. And I didn't say a word about you and she didn't ask."

"Oh she knows."

"Damn right she knows."

"I don't think she cares." You stared at us with your frightened, sorrowful, it's-all-over-now eyes. "The way she looked, she didn't look like she wanted to talk to anybody she knew ever again."

"I can see that."

"I can see that, too."

"So what happened exactly?"

"I just told you. I should really get up there and see the kids."

"We've got it covered. Besides, your daughter asked for a few minutes. So where you been?"

"Trying to find her, of course. When I told her, first she tried to . . . she tried to talk, then she just stopped and she got up and she just started clubbing me, really pounding me just like she had every right to and just like I deserved; she hit me so hard I fell off the chair. Then she ran from the café—I'd managed to sit her down at a café. I had to pay, and then I ran after her. I kept thinking I was seeing her but the truth was I don't think I ever saw her. Look, I've got to get up there." You pushed past us and unlocked the door. We looked at each other and shrugged. We followed you in and up the stairs.

"You're not going to say anything to the kids, are you?"

"I don't know what I'm going to say."

"You've got two teenaged daughters, for god's sake."

"My daughters see right through me." You were climbing the stairs and we could literally see the tears dropping at your feet. "Oh god."

"It doesn't have to be so intense, man."

"Just take it easy up there, okay? Of course they're your kids and everything, but you need to relax so you can see it."

"Sure," you said. You were sobbing.

"Man, I thought this was a comedy we were in."

"A comedy about this? Right now this is like a comedy about torture. It can't work. I know it wants to make some kind of social commentary, like, look, this is okay in other cultures and the fact that it's not okay in ours says something fucked-up about our culture, not about us. But the culture we're in isn't going to buy that, which is the whole circular problem. Besides that, it's pretty clear we all want to stay with our wives and we're all territorial as hell about them, for whatever reason. So it's not like we have any courage or actual enlightened open-mindedness or anything. It will just seem nonsensical and immoral and hypocritical. Truthful, honest, but dead in the water. Like we would be if our wives found out. Like our boy here is. He is absolutely fucking dead in the water."

At the door ahead of us, you were weeping and unable to speak at the door.

"Man, you are a cold-hearted pessimist."

"I'm a realist. That's the military."

"Again?"

"Again."

"In advertising we call that AFB. We'd assess a product absolutely fact-based, and then we'd figure out how to alter, manipulate, contextualize, and omit without any actual illegal distortion."

"Tell me something I don't know."

"Fuck you."

"Fuck you."

We laughed. You make somebody really nervous and they will laugh like a fucking hyena.

"Look, man, I know it seems like everything has come to an awful terminal point here, but would you open the door? We've got to take a leak."

You wiped your eyes with an elbow and opened the door.

Inside it was so dark it was like we were venturing into the inner chamber of someone's head, right past the skull and into the really dark matter.

"Shh."

You stepped cautiously in and refrained from turning on any light. Behind us, we shut the door.

"Are they really in here?" you said tentatively.

"Unless they climbed up the fire escape and fled from the roof, they're really in here."

"I'm taking a leak," the other guy said, and felt his way through the kitchen and began bumping down the hall. Soon a door opened and shut and we could hear a light click on and him pissing in the bowl.

"So now what?" you said.

"The truth is an evil path."

You sat on the sofa in the dark. Then you stood up. "You think she'll come back?"

"How the hell would I know? She's your wife. But you've humiliated and disgusted her and called everything into question. She's got to be thinking about money, her safety, the kids. She'll come back for the kids. But you, you might never see her again."

"I might never see her again," you repeated dumbly.

"If you're lucky."

"I did this to start over. I did this so she could know what I was, find some way to exact satisfaction if she hadn't already, and we could begin again like we were naked before god—"

"You don't even believe in god. Whereas I actually do."

"You know what I mean. Instead I've destroyed everything."

"Of course you have. As I told you you would. One affair, that's something some people could forgive or figure out a way to resolve. Though from my perspective I doubt anybody ever has just one affair. That's like one potato chip or one drink or one Seconal. You had to give her the whole nine yards and so you are done. My advice to you is get what you can from your bank account and your communal stuff, right now, because you won't have that ability much longer. And don't be obvious about it, because if she wants to she could probably have even the shirt off your back."

"I don't care," you said. "I don't want anything. I don't deserve anything." You looked around in the dark. "I thought you said my daughter was going to let you in."

"She was. She probably forgot or was hoping we'd go away. She said she'd forgotten we were down there."

You got up. "I'd better—"

"Don't. You are not ready, and they're resting. And besides that, I can tell you that we don't want to be here when you do. Where the hell is our guy anyway?"

"I'm here," he said, coming out slowly from the dark. "You can't see a damn thing with all the lights off. I'm gathering we ought to push off?"

"Exactly."

We both clapped you on the shoulder.

"What's done is done. And what we have to deal with, we'll deal with. And if you have ruined us, we'll deal with that, too."

"I know," you said, sniffling.

"It's one life, you know? If you take it too seriously, you'll lose it a lot sooner than you think."

"Okay."

We left you in the dark, like a mold that needed more time to grow, like a barely dead body in its crypt. Who knew what anyone would see when next they opened the door? On the street, once far enough away, we dialed our wives and informed them that you had returned, that still we knew nothing, that we refused to speculate, and we were going to stop for a real bite to eat. We looked at each other and grinned. That wasn't a new one, and it did always work. The only problem was that we'd have to go a little hungry. But that was nothing compared to the problem of you.

"Someplace new, perhaps?"

"Wherever we choose is going to be pretty quiet."

"Hot Spices?"

"I've heard of it. You been?"

"Never."

"Then it'll be something different."

For a moment we could feel like we were you back in the day, walking from your row house, taking in the quaint useless shops and that fine Mexican restaurant, crossing the boulevard and in the distance glimpsing the different light from the harbor, standing in front of the ornate art museum with its pillars and gargoyles and stained glass. The cab rolled up promptly just like it would have for you, and we got in, feeling like the last free men on earth, and told the driver the cross streets we needed. He nodded—like they all did—as if he knew. Ninety-eight brothels, and if you'd been a cabbie for ten or a dozen years, maybe you did know. Ninety-eight brothels and a dozen marquee department stores and a hundred really good restaurants and five art museums and a zoo and four major parks and maybe a hundred and fifty brand-name or designer clothing stores and sixty-seven truly historic bars and twenty-nine first-class hotels and an underground grid of shopping and eating and drinking for the winter months and five sections of waterfront for the summer months and four different train stations and an airport with six different termi-nals—you could probably keep track, so that when two guys of a certain look and a certain age got into your cab and gave you an obscure set of cross streets, despite their attempt to veil the nature of their destination, you likely did know. The cabbie grunted indifferently and snapped on his radio. It was hard to believe there were any indifferent people in such a beautiful frantic city.

We watched some of it pass by. Dusty orange trees refract-ing white street lights, teenagers smoking cigarettes on a cor-ner, the boys eyeing the girls and the girls eyeing the boys as if, given the right move, they might all instantly succumb to one another, a woman bending over to lock the grate into place at a dress shop, her jeans riding down, her bright red thong putting on a show.

"You see that?"

"I saw it."

As we climbed the stairs to Hot Spices someone was de-scending, the door closing behind him. He looked like a nor-mal guy between appointments, run ragged by all of his re-sponsibilities, just trying to catch a break. He was buttoning his shirt as he hurried down the steps. He kept his eyes on the street below as if we weren't there, as if it weren't possible there could be any people between here and there, his expression as serious and remote as a physician's. We walled ourselves off from the other guy in much the same way; even when we went in together we walled ourselves off, first to determine our selection, and then because we were going in there to make only one thing happen and that did take some concentration, and afterward to get out of there it was necessary to retain some focus or we just might lose ourselves.

It was a little hard to believe we were going inside, after what most of the night had already been. We rang the bell, were let in, were led to a room, and the parade began. A baker's dozen, the quantity not bad for a Monday night, the quality low to medium, but we were already there, so what were we going to do? We scrutinized our annotations on the notepads that had thoughtfully been left for us, we muttered to each other our specific concerns, we smiled sadly or insincerely at our mutual awkwardness. The hostess returned with our drinks and asked for our choices. We hesitated; a moment like this was so truly agonizing and just bad form.

"I'm afraid," we said, "we just can't."

"Gentlemen," she said. "It is not a problem. Perhaps another time."

"Yes, another time. Can we at least pay you something for the drinks?"

"You haven't touched them, gentlemen," she said, "so really it is not necessary."

Ten minutes later, in a bar two streets over, we agreed it had been difficult to concentrate. Was it the image of your children or the image of you or the image of your wife fleeing unhappily somewhere within the city? It was true that occasionally there could be a kind of ennui at one of these reflective moments, and we sat there, drinking ginger ale of all things, and picking at tiny barrel-shaped pickles and a plate of potato chips. We sat there wordlessly wondering at the momentary depression that had settled over us.

"That place sucked."

"I know. So we won't ever go back."

"Never."

That seemed to clear the air, or at least stir it out of its sad stagnancy.

"How many do you think we have left?"

"I told you, probably the captain used to know for certain, but if I had to guess, I'd say seventy-three."

"Man, we are obsessed."

"There are worse things to obsess about."

"That's for damn sure."

We ordered cocktails and a plate of burger sliders.

"Man, I thought that place was supposed to be so hot."

"Maybe we got the weak rotation."

"Thirteen girls and all of them were mediocre? No way."

"At least the price wasn't so bad."

"That's true, that's true. Here's to you, man."

We lifted our glasses. "I'd rather we toasted the captain."

"The captain who's steering us into an iceberg?"

"The captain who's hit his own iceberg while the rest of us are still free to steer our course."

We gulped our drinks.

"That's the million-dollar question."

"It's not a question. It is the actual state of things. Our phones aren't ringing off the hook, and my guess is this will be an internal humiliation, the kind you keep to yourself rather than spread around, and why? I can only say I sense this from her reaction thus far. All signs are encouraging, and while we might need to lay low for a while—this evening notwithstanding—I have every hope our society will endure, and I am confident enough to say so."

We leaned in and tapped glasses.

"Now that I can drink to. That and these sliders."

They were the kind you could eat in one wolfish bite if you were motivated, juicy with ketchup and some chopped onions and mustard and a patina of some kind of sharp cheese, gorgonzola or blue. We cut the third carefully in half and ordered another round of cocktails. If we timed it right, we'd reach our homes as everyone was falling asleep and be ourselves able to hit the sack in a relatively good mood. After the kind of day today had been, that was saying something. We sat there grinning at each other.

"I could almost try another one."

We checked our watches. "I know. I know."

"Do you want to?"

"My Cialis is good for another three hours. I don't see why not."

"Seventy-six?"

"Seventy-six."

We paid and hurried the five blocks to Seventy-six. Ahead of us were two tourist guys obviously hunting for it, but there were two Seventy-sixes and you had to know which one. Gleefully we went in ahead of them, and they were held behind while we were taken to the lounge, that beautifully appointed contemporary room with the golden vinyl banquette along three walls and the Scandinavian blond wood bar backed by fluorescently lit tiers and tiers of bottles.

"Sit, gentlemen, and I will bring in the girls."

She left while we sat together in the absolute middle of the banquette. When she returned she stood in the doorway, and each girl walked in as if on a meticulously timed conveyor belt. The hostess called out their names as if she were scrolling down a class roster. "Giselle . . . Marguerite . . . Imma . . . Toulouse . . . Sanya . . . Mimosa . . . Cinnamon." We kissed each one, and each one took a seat on the banquette, until the entire banquette was full with fourteen or fifteen girls.

"Gentlemen?" the hostess said.

He leaned close. "I know which one I'm having. That little Colombian that I told you about. She won't quit. And that one," he pointed discreetly to a young, too-thin blonde almost hiding as she leaned far back against the banquette, "that was the one who curled her fist and made him sad."

"Then I'll do her. I'll do her for him."

"That's the spirit."

"Gentlemen?"

"Carmella."

"Ludvika."

The other girls rose and touched their colleagues on the shoulder with a congratulatory and chatty patter, and immediately departed. Carmella came and corralled our guy, and Ludvika hung back a bit but eventually led the way. The rooms still seemed brand new, not a stain or an unraveled thread in sight. She took the drink order and returned with that and a set of sheets and got everything ready. We kept the light on, and in her face you could see that she was every bit the nineteen that she claimed, despite her freckles and hint of a natural blush, and when she turned over onto her tummy and we did it that way, her hands clenched into fists and she gave a little moan and then another and another. She was really too thin, bony even, but she was pure for this kind of thing, new to this kind of thing, and while she might have been good at hiding herself in a line-up, she had no idea how to hide herself in bed; she hadn't mastered the art that some of them had of not being there, or of being there but not with you, one or the other. She was more than okay, and it was easy then to thank god for Cialis and for giving it all a second chance tonight. It was easy to finish.

"Okay?" she said, looking back up from the pillow, so that it was true you could see her as a child, a five-year-old say, but an infant? That seemed excessive.

"Okay."

"You want shower?"

"Sure."

We showered, and she laughed as she scrubbed, obviously happy to be past the hard work.

"I know another one of your guys."

"You do?" she said. "I'm pretty new."

"Yes, a nice guy. Probably too nice a guy. He said you made him sad."

"Oh, I remember him." Her hand reached to her mouth as if to stifle a burp or a giggle. "He was a very serious one, right?"

"That's him."

"I only saw him once. One of my first nights here."

"He liked you a lot."

She looked perplexed. "Then why hasn't he come back?"

"He got . . . conflicted. He has a wife, kids—"

"All you guys have wife and kids."

"He said you reminded him of his kids when they were just babies. The way you . . . the way you clench your fists."

"Ach." She looked vexed. "That just means I'm doing fine."

We both looked at her free hand and she clenched it into a fist.

"Like that?" she said.

"Like that."

She took the shower nozzle and sprayed her fist with it, then sprayed both of us all over. We laughed.

"You've done this before here, though?"

"Of course."

"Since?"

"Since I don't know when."

A lot of these questions were bad form, but it was hard to resist with her, because while it could be argued that our girls were like all the girls, she was most like all the girls of anybody in a long while.

"Are you clean?"

"Yes."

We got dressed and met at the door, where she picked up the phone and waited and waited.

"It's a pretty busy night," she said, "even if it's Monday."

"It's the new hot place."

"You should have seen the weekend. Friday. And Saturday—Saturday it was ringing the whole time and marching in and out of the bar the whole time. On Saturday even my feet were tired. But I'm not complaining. This place is new and fresh, and going in there all at once is not a bad idea, the way we all get to be together before we separate."

We looked at the quiet phone. "And security is pretty good?"

"The best. We've got a couple big guys hanging out in the basement, and they could be up here like that." She snapped her fingers; she was seeming older by the minute. "Of course, they haven't had to. It's a great town to work in. It sure beats where I was last."

"Where was that?"

"_____."

"_____."

The door buzzed and we were let out. In the hallway we could hear our guy hollering, "Is that you? Don't leave without me! This chick just won't let me out just yet."

We said our good-byes and she walked back down the hall and the hostess smiled and gestured toward a small waiting room.

"You can wait for your friend in here. Was everything okay?"

"Perfect."

There were a few sports magazines and a bucket of ice and fresh glasses and a pitcher of water. The TV showed a basketball game. The walls breathed a kind of contentment. Then our guy stuck his grinning wet head in the doorway. "You ready?"

As we headed out, more guys were coming in. We glanced at our watches. One on a Tuesday morning.

"Damn it's late," he said.

"Service was slow."

"We had to wait for a table."

"Exactly."

Two cabs waited at the corner.

"Man, everyone knows about this place."

We shook hands.

"I'll see you soon."

"Not if I see you first."

On the way home, in the first silence of the past day, it was easy to think of the good times we'd all had this spring—the trip in May to the other coast that we haven't even talked about yet, when you led us to a couple of those dinner bars where the girls looked like they were dressed for a prom or a debutante ball, and negotiations were actually complicated and we had to concentrate to keep track of the sliding scale and the differential and the two-for-the-price-of-one-and-a-half, as if we were on the floor of the stock market. They had great girls over there, though while yours insisted she was nineteen we all thought her sixteen at best, and her contention that she was saving up to return to Brazil to become a veterinarian seemed specious. Afterward when we told you this you were flustered, because if you'd done someone your own kid's age that was a signifier. There were so many ways you were looking to crucify yourself. But you couldn't stop. None of us could. It was too fun, too easy, too strange, too enticing, too much like a dream. What happened when an inexhaustible supply met an inexhaustible demand? This happened.

And then, on the plane ride back, we could see below us the shadow of the plane on the clouds and it was a gecko. And then we were in the clouds and the ride roughened; we were tossed and bumped as the plane rocked and skittered. It seemed to us then that every flight we'd ever been on had its moments of absolute authority and sheer uncertainty, moments when we knew we couldn't possibly drop from the sky and moments when we were sure that that was the next thing that would happen.

In the condo the kids were asleep and the wife was snoring that soft sad tone that probably wives everywhere sang when they were left to fall asleep alone, and perhaps too it contained a note of happiness or relief that we couldn't even detect. It was peaceful to remember the way it was before we were married, when she gave whatever was wanted and apparently enjoyed it, and how once that paper was signed, it all changed, but that was a different story. Marriage was the first wrong piece of the puzzle, the fatal flaw of the design, the weak foundation, the problematic cornerstone. Was there a metaphor that did justice to what it was? It was the essential irreconcilable contradiction between the desire for the new and the unknowable and the instinct for the permanent and the familiar. Why would anyone limit himself when time itself was limited, when the older you got the more quickly it all rushed past you? Ours was just one more approach in the constant struggle to protract time, and who knew if that wasn't what our wives were contemplating or doing, too. It wasn't easy to fall asleep thinking like this, the clock counting down the lost opportunity for rest, a chance before it all began again—the morning riot, herding the kids into the car, the business hours across eight or nine time zones, the narrow domesticated evening that awaited not like some kind of soothing cocoon but like a straitjacket cinched tight with a padlock. Why ever would anyone sign that paper?

The phone rang the next morning with the car nosing in traffic and the instinct was to think it was the wife but of course it was you.

"So where are they?" you said.

"Who?"

"My kids. Where are my kids? I just woke up and there's no one here. Where are they?"

"Maybe your wife slipped in and took them to school."

"And I slept through that? In this place?"

"You're physically and mentally exhausted. You could probably have slept through a truck crashing into your living room." The phone beeped a serious reminder. "I've got a conference call. Check with the schools. We'll talk in thirty."

There was the conference call and there was parking the car in the overpriced garage and there was the trudge up into the office and the examination of messages and the happy-face greeting with the hot but unfruitful secretary, and then e-mail and voicemail and faxes, it was always amazing how many words had to be expended to make a little money, and the phone kept beeping your impatience, but really, old friend, there was no time. Finally, past noon, before lunch, a moment announced itself.

"So did you locate them?"

"No."

"No?"

"Absolutely no."

"Is there anything missing?"

"The kids' favorite blankets and stuffed animals."

"Then she took them. Have you checked to see what's left in your bank account?"

"Two hundred."

"Two hundred from?"

"Nineteen thousand."

"That should last them a few weeks. You could probably track them by the credit card after that. Any idea where they went?"

"Somewhere temperate. Somewhere she doesn't know anybody."

"Both good guesses. So what do you want to do? This couldn't have been unexpected, you know."

"I don't know."

"Well, I hate to do this, but I'll loan you some money. Then you can open a new bank account. Do you understand?"

"Yes. I mean, thank you."

"Don't mention it. Besides, you haven't seen my rates. I'll have my secretary draw up the terms. Can you come by around four?"

"Around four," you repeated. "Yes, of course. And thank you again."

The phone sank back into its place and the window still offered the sea. A note on the desk from the unrealized secretary confirmed that the lawyer wanted to have lunch. There was always lunch, wasn't there. Like the old song, *Things are never as bad as they can be, and at least there is always lunch*. In our city it meant wine and laughter and more wine and the escalation of shared confidences until the relationship was deep enough to make some real money for everyone involved. The lawyer closed the deals and the lawyer wanted to have lunch, so there had to be lunch. Lunch some other time was preferable, but it was not possible. The only thing possible was lunch.

It was at a typical modernist minimalist wine bar restaurant mired in the middle of the city and the one innovation it offered was a recessed wine chiller at each table setting, as if every patron should order his own bottle of wine and as if every wine had to be chilled. But the magic didn't stop there, we learned as we dutifully listened to our waiter, for each individual wine chiller had its own electronic temperature settings and these ranged in calibration from bold red to soft red to buttery white to grassy white to the sparkling wines. Needless to say, we felt obliged to order a bottle of wine apiece to test this pathetic gimmick for ourselves.

"You will not be disappointed," the waiter said, his face frozen in a seriousness of purpose that did not allow for a hint of irony, or a recognition of the utterly cheesy posturing to which he was restricting himself. We laughed so hard we nearly fell out of our chairs.

As we sipped our perfectly chilled wines and indeed marveled at just how spectacular they were, in accordance with the tradition and the practice of the city we did not mention business at all, but, as if on a first date, we discussed our personal trajectories and our families and our friendships, our philosophies and our passions, our avocations and other tangential interests, our cars and our homes, our recent vacations and our favorite destinations, until before long we were sliding in such facts—as men sometimes did—as our favorite positions and our favorite places to get some. While it was not unusual to find such an instant like-minded confederate so close at hand, it was not expected either, and there followed an excited exchange of information as if we were frantically trying to top each other with our respective accumulations of knowledge. There was no real moment as yet to mention your case, though it was hard not to look for it, and besides, as anyone would instantly know, you were a lost cause. What man confessed everything and expected anything but the abject collapse of the world as he knew it? Still, it could not be resisted.

"I have this friend," it began.

The lawyer listened raptly; by now we were on our third and fourth bottles of wine—our curiosity regarding the range and depth of the gimmick having extended itself to something of an obsession, which of course was its intended effect—and certainly some details were muddled and others obfuscated to protect the guilty, something we were all expert at, and at the end, once the story had reached its current impasse, the lawyer leaned back, squeezed the bridge of his nose between his thumb and forefinger as if to pinch out some ultimate thought, and pronounced, "If I know anything, whatever you do—and even if you really do need to lend him the money— whatever you do, there must be no paper between you."

"But that would mean—"

"An undocumented loan. You're going to loan him— what—twenty thousand. Twenty thousand to you is like two hundred to most people. And obviously his character is such, I don't see him welshing on it, or whatever the colloquial abomination is. Myself, I am deep in foreclosure."

"That goes against everything my father ever taught me."

"Sometimes it is not possible to follow a father's advice. A father's advice can be limited in its capacity to embrace the complexity of modern life. Even if, as we both know, what we're engaged in is not modern at all, but has its roots in the most ancient civilizations. Money, sex—the vagaries and spectrums of these types of interactions and the arenas in which they are played—this is all ancient matter. So, regardless, yes. An undocumented loan."

"I have never—"

"Look, you know me as a thoughtful man who understands the law and knows how to navigate it. But I am also someone who senses that in reality there are no laws, there are only principles, and then what must happen is that these applicable principles must be assessed against each other and one must proceed accordingly. It is my assessment that any risk you are taking with this relatively small undocumented loan is outweighed by the risk you might be taking in actually documenting the loan."

"I am not a two-year-old, you know." The china and silverware clanked between us uncomfortably. "I know exactly what you are saying."

"Then good. It's settled."

When you arrived at precisely five minutes to four, in this city where being late is not only a common practice but also a requisite etiquette, we stood for a while looking out the window at the boats, the bathers on the waterfront; another beautiful day in paradise, as we liked to say.

"It is beautiful," you said.

"I have bad news and good news, captain. I'm not going to loan you the money, but I am going to give it to you."

"I can't accept that," you said.

"You'll have to. I am of the persuasion that any business between real friends is never a good idea. So we must proceed in a more—well, I don't want to say charitable—in a more celebratory fashion. I am giving you this gift to celebrate the occasion of your liberation. You're a free man now, captain, and even though you might not feel like it at this moment, trust me when I say it is something to celebrate."

"I will pay you back," you said.

"If you pay me back you are returning a gift, and that would mean the end of our friendship."

We looked each other in the eye. Yours were red-rimmed, as if you'd been soaking them in chlorine.

"You're kidding," you said.

"I'm dead serious."

You smiled tentatively, trying to land on something. "Then I'll get you a gift in a return."

"Somehow, I knew you'd say that." We shook hands, and in yours you found the twenty thousand in a small tight roll of five hundreds. "Now take that to the bank."

You looked hard at the money. "Your lawyer made you do this."

"Exactly."

"But why?"

"Something about one risk far outweighing another. Have I ever mentioned I quit law school after just one year?"

You laughed. "Many times. And my mother signed me up to see five different shrinks, and I never showed up at any of them."

"She must have been pissed."

"Still is."

The one week she visited you here, you would not let any of us meet her. Your wife's father we'd all seen so often that we felt the same way about him that you did. It was hard to believe men like us had parents, let alone in-laws, but we did.

"Take care, captain. And call when you're up to it."

"I will."

You left, the sag in your shoulders an indicator of things to come, the twenty thousand in your pocket like a bottle of water for a drowning man. Imagine if none of us ever had the money. Would there even have been affairs, for wasn't the swagger of our success, the muscular rise of our stock, a good part of what attracted them to us in the first place? Sure, there were women who sought the occasional reclamation project, but these were

more often than not the kind resulting from aesthetic despair
and alienation rather than actual financial penury. The women
who gravitated toward us gratis were women who smelled success and wanted to baste themselves with it. Think of our advertising guy who only had to work two hours a week, or dude
guy, who apparently didn't have to work at all and could careen
drunkenly all night through the city without bothering to notice how much he spent. Those guys drove women crazy.

Among wealth, dominance, and accomplishment, which
did you seek the most avidly?

Most of us were about the wealth, because with money
came everything. You valued accomplishment the most, captain. You valued being called captain! But you'd been over-
thrown by your own conscience. You, who had always wanted
to become a leader of men, had become in name only the leader of the wrong kind of men, and though we liked to joke that
you were leading us into battle, the ultimate resistance was
never in those bars and those back rooms, but waiting in our
minds and our own rooms, and these battles you had lost. You
had lost them and you had lost yourself, and there was nothing to be done, not a damn thing, and it was all your doing
and who knew how many times we had told you that the only
possible strategy, the only possible mode of survival, was to
keep it to yourself. First you couldn't handle the greed (because
that was what we all were; greedy, greedy bastards, and you as
the least monied were not surprisingly the most greedy), and
then you couldn't handle the anxiety. You saw her face fall to
that untouched dessert plate, you heard her utter those words
of intense recognition and dismay, *But now, but now*, and you
were practically done. Were we angry? We were shocked, but
we shouldn't have been, because you were always the serious
one. We were worried, but we shouldn't have been, because as

you sank you clutched at the code, determined to sink alone and this ironically determined to make your poor wife feel that she too was alone, though she had all the company in the world. Where the sudden ignition of your guilt could have torched a half dozen homes, you were determined to limit the destruction to the absolute incineration of just a single isolated family. As Tuesday gave way to Wednesday and then Thursday, we could see that. Our wives did not look upon us with any more suspicion than usual, our children did not shy from us despite the sudden and mysterious absence of yours from soccer, on the fields the head of the league maintained his constant air of obsequiousness and distraction. Nothing changed, except for you. We sent one another blandly puzzled texts—any news? hear anything?—and we kept an ear out for any sound of you. From time to time we could hear our wives speculating about the sudden vanishing act, and from time to time at their urging we checked in with you, but there was never an answer and there wasn't even a voicemail prompt. A few of us stopped by the row house now and again, but the windows were always shuttered and from the street we could hear the hollow echo all through the building when we rang the bell. We could only imagine what was taking place in this riot of silence—were you on their trail, were delicate negotiations evolving, were lawyers involved—and all the inscrutable secretary at the soccer league office would offer was that word had been sent—*word had been sent*—that the children had been withdrawn just ten days short of the season's end.

To be honest, it was a little like having a tumor removed, for even if all of our families were malignancies harbored within some small or large societal body, yours was the only tumor to symptomize and to suggest metastasis, and then, if your mass had indeed been so deftly and fully excised and all margins were proving negative, then how otherwise were we to take it, except to accept our good fortune and grasp at whatever life there was because certainly it trumped the known alternative? Did we feel guilty? Of course. But somehow too—and this is harder to articulate—we felt innocent, as if misguided or reckless or third-party acts of exposure were the sole determination of anyone's guilt.

While the effects of your absence lingered like a seasonal climate, certain to end sometime but one never knew exactly when, we remained vigilant. Whatever drove us—indifference, neglect, lust—to become who we had become was still a component of our everyday lives, and we had to keep ourselves in check while at the same time maintaining constant watch on the larger situation. Would your cautionary tale prove indispensable or even instructive? In fairness to an accurate history of sex, no. It wouldn't even stand the test of time. Every week the national newspapers were rife with yet another story of the famous caught in the salacious, and within a year or two at most you could turn on the television to find that same person basking in the warmth garnered from earnest gestures of apparent self-revelation and self-expiation. The public's appetite for your own tale would have been relatively small, and, thanks to your discretion, most of those who might have been interested didn't even know what it was. Besides, it had gotten to be summer, time to leave the brothels behind and take our families back home to pay homage to the children's grandparents and whatever it was we had escaped, big-box stores and retail outlets and frilly suburban streets and city sidewalks trod by the trapped and the bored. For a whole month we were further undone and disconnected by itineraries that never overlapped, so that we were once again just men with their offspring-centered, wife-run households, caught in the numbing cycle of attraction-hunting, half-hearted discipline, and television. By the time late July arrived with its promise of mid-summer festivities and doldrums, the threat of anything arising from you had faded to something like a patch of dust in a barely inhabited room, easily addressed at any first glance. *Whatever happened to them? Who knew, but he was an odd guy.*

At last four or five of us were sitting in a row at the bar at Girls, dillydallying with our overpriced drinks, eyeing the room's contents, enjoying the shock of sudden reentry after nine or ten long weeks out of circulation, the girls approaching in waves, our small talk creaking with rust.

"Why haven't you come around in so long?"

"Don't you want to buy me a drink?"

"Come on, honey, the room's waiting."

We smirked and smiled and grinned, reacquiring our skill of discernment.

"Your friend was by the other night. The serious one, you know? He didn't even close."

"You saw him?"

"He sat right there," a blonde said, a blonde we'd all tried. "He didn't say nothing. He had maybe one drink. He sat with his head in his hands for maybe an hour. We all asked if he was okay. He wouldn't even take his sunglasses off. One of us even offered—you know—something outside on the side. He didn't want nothing."

"It's true." A redhead nodded. "What's up with him anyway?" We told her.

"Well, so he is serious. That's kind of attractive, you know. And anyway, so what's the big deal?"

We sat there, drinking over that. What was it about the practice of sex that we couldn't get right, that we couldn't get the whole world to agree on?

"He wasn't getting any at home," the redhead continued. Ivonya, that was her name. "None of you guys are. And if you are, it isn't enough. Or you want something a little bit different. It's like food, you know? You're not going to eat in the same restaurant every day of your life. And the fact that you've chosen to come to professionals says something not only about your investment in the process but also your commitment to your families. Anyway that's what I think, and I've been doing this for a while now."

"And exactly how long is that?" one of us asked. All of us wanted her; you could feel it.

"Thirteen months," she said.

"That's what you said four months ago."

She touched dude guy's hair very lightly, and we all felt the thrill of it. "You've got five minutes, boys, and then we have to move on."

"You're a regular intellectual," dude guy said, moving this way and that, getting her hand to drop here and there.

"I know," she said, obliging him, cracking her gum. "It's a turn-on."

It all felt too normal. It was a pick-up bar where everyone could pick up. God it was good to be back. We ordered more drinks and let the wave of her crash past us. It was one of those nights when we were in it for the long haul, when we were determined to engage every girl there, when we were going to take all the time in the world even if it meant stirring the milkshake.

"I think we did a good job laying low."

"It was pretty severe there for a while."

"Were you ever really worried?"

"Of course I was worried. I kept looking around my house as if that would be the last time we'd all be in it."

"That's what he used to say. He didn't give us up, though."

"He sure didn't."

"To the captain."

"To the captain!"

All over the bar glasses seemed to be chiming, and out of the fog of cigarette smoke a new girl seemed to emerge every minute. There were two bartenders, then three, and soon you couldn't walk anywhere, it was so jammed, and the line for the rooms was a dozen couples deep.

"I've never seen it this mobbed."

"Must be the economy's finally picking up."

"And it's tourist season."

"Ah, tourist season." We all sagely nodded. "The bastards."

"I can't stand how they know where to go right away whereas it took us—"

"Exactly."

We watched them in their khaki shorts and polo shirts. At least they diluted the creep factor. They all had whitened teeth and new haircuts. Even their sandals were expensive. You could tell they were players. There were so many of them the waves had stopped entirely and movement was stalled as if this were a mob being filtered into an arena for an athletic event. It was kind of weird.

"There are probably fifty girls tonight, and it's still not enough."

"People are going to start getting nasty."

"Exactly."

We scrutinized the place for any sign of trouble. A couple of familiar-looking gangster types seemed perfectly relaxed as they hunched over their drinks and cigarettes amidst the bedlam. The tourists appeared to be utterly polite. And the guy out front did frisk everyone on the way in.

"I think everyone is pretty secure in the knowledge that they're all going to get some."

"A place like this, they never want any trouble."

"It's the number one mid-level place in town. It has a kind of very public aspect that everyone has to trust. This place does not fuck up. That guy out front wears an earpiece, for Christ's sake."

"I love that guy."

"I do, too."

"So tell me something, dude," dude guy shouted over the din. "And I mean this. This is something I have never figured out. Is this legal or not?"

"Not for our marriages, it isn't."

"But in the general sense, it's not illegal," the ad guy said. "Read the municipal laws, man. It is not legal to solicit on the street. But the law says nothing about soliciting in a private venue, such as a club or a privately owned bar. It's a brilliant act of omission. So we're not illegal, but we're probably not terribly legal either."

"Fantastic."

"You seriously didn't know?"

"I seriously didn't know."

"I just think it's a little late to be having this discussion."

"The fact that my wife doesn't ask any questions, that's the big thing."

"Maybe she doesn't want *you* asking any questions."

"Of course. That makes sense. But still."

"Why do you think he did it?"

"What?"

"Why do you think he told his wife?"

"He wanted them to be innocent again."

"Oh, dude, we're never innocent."

"I know."

"When was the last time you ever felt innocent?"

"I guess when I first came out of my mother, but of course I can't remember that."

"Exactly."

"Hey, that's my line."

"After a while, we all start talking like each other."

"Sure."

"I still can't believe he told her."

"He just cracked, dude guy. People do."

"Dude guy?"

"Sorry, what the hell am I supposed to be calling you again?"

"I'm Connor, dude. I've been Connor ever since we started coming here. And you're Ronald."

"I am indeed."

"And he's Jack. And he's Ray. And that dark bastard over there is Winston."

"Exactly."

"You don't think we're being a bit paranoid by keeping up this fake shit, do you?"

"No way." A bunch of us shook our heads. "You heard Ivonya talking about the captain. The girls talk."

"That they do."

"I remember I came in here once and she told me you were in the night before, she described you down to your birthmark, and she said, 'His name's Connor, isn't it?'"

"Jesus."

"It's not good. But it's going to be all right."

"I'm really not the paranoid type. And like I said, my wife doesn't ask any questions."

"That's a good wife."

"I wish I could stop." He smiled sadly and then he grinned. "I guess we're all addicted."

"We just want to have fun before we die."

"Okay."

"Exactly."

"Do you think monogamy is possible?"

"No. Or it's possible for some people, but they're definitely not us and they're definitely in the minority."

"You sure about that?"

"It's what history and all the statistics tell us."

"Okay."

"I'm not making it up."

"Exactly." He was grinning again.

"I told you not to say that."

"That's not what you said. You said it was your line—"

"And that means not to say it."

"Geez, you said it would get nasty, but I didn't think you meant it about yourself."

"Look." We quickly took a sip from our drinks. "I could have you killed like that if I wanted. The fact that I haven't says something wonderful about our friendship."

"Ah, your military days again." Dude guy sighed. "Honestly, it sounds like it did you more harm than good."

"Maybe so. All I know is I have a pretty good life now."

"We all do, dude. We live here!"

"Another round?"

"Fuck, yeah."

There were still five of us. Four or five of us. And it was nearing two o'clock. You could begin to discern spaces around the bar, free air, a girl here or there recovering. It had to be a lot of work to keep all these men happy. It wasn't exactly something that stirred the loins to see them like this in between romps or clients or whatever you wanted to call them. The happiest we'd all been was when we were early at places, and everyone was so fresh and shiny it was like getting to the produce stand first. We looked around at the smoky, sweaty mess of our favorite large-scale brothel. Two thirty, two forty-five, three, and every girl would have been unimaginably crusty if they all didn't wash like seals.

"Should we move on?"

"Gentlemen, it is now or never."

Our first time out in weeks and weeks and we had waited so long, culled so long, that it was no longer possible. Even the Cialis had probably worn off.

"I see an old favorite."

"Me too."

We nodded and waved and in a moment were once again surrounded.

"Shall we?"

"We shall."

Outside afterward in the short summer night, with the seam of dawn already breaking apart the sky, we agreed it had been worth it—not the wait, but the late plunge. Perhaps it was because the girls could see the end of their own long night, knowing that we would be the last ones, that they gave themselves more fully, not quite GFE but for that place, where so much of it was public and where the walls were so thin, as close as we could imagine they would ever get to it. Mouthy, tonguey, tender kisses, a sleepy ease and openness, slurred murmurings instead of the too crisp *Oh baby baby*, an unrehearsed, nearly wordless quality. We were all performers, of course, and we all knew that every interaction was a performance. But still. But still.

"But still it was kind of soupy."

"Don't go there, dude. Don't go there."

We laughed and pounded each other on the back and climbed into a few taxis between us. As we were carried our separate ways into the Heights, our drivers tapped their horns at each other. The sun was rising now, suddenly fast.

That summer morning the doorman called up to the condo to say we had a visitor, a Ms. _____, the name so garbled that neither of us with our caked weekend brains could discern even remotely whom he might be talking about. We looked at each other and shrugged. It was nearly noon, the children were still in their pajamas, we'd missed church for the sixteenth consecutive Sunday since Easter, and a sultry air seemed to press through the shut windows into our refrigerated rooms.

"Send her on up, we guess."

We both went to the door, opened it, and waited for the elevator to deliver her.

She emerged in a stylish linen pant suit, her face a bit flushed from the heat, her short, bright blonde hair moussed enough to withstand the humidity. She looked strangely familiar.

"Hello," she said.

"Are you looking for us?"

She shook both our hands formally, her own a bit damp, but not distastefully so. It must have been nearly a hundred out. It was too hot even for the beach. You could tell all this just by looking at her.

She introduced herself as your wife's sister.

"Really?" We looked at each other and swallowed any impolite surprise. "Well, come in, come in. You do look very familiar. And how is your sister doing?"

"How is my sister doing?" she said, as she sat on the couch and we hurried to get out drinks and snacks. "I was hoping you could tell me. Neither my father or I have heard anything from her since the middle of June."

"The middle of June," we both repeated.

"I got your name from the secretary of the soccer league. She said you all were closest with the family, and perhaps you'd know something. She herself hadn't heard anything since they withdrew the children."

"Have you tried her husband?"

"My father, who is not well, and I have tried everything. It's like they disappeared off the face of the earth. You're my last stop before I go to the police, which is frankly something we've been resisting since it seems so radical." She took a sip from her glass of iced tea. "I mean, there's no sign of his business or hers. Everyone's telling me they must be on vacation somewhere, but nobody's cell phone is picking up and the people on their block say they haven't seen them in more than two months. If you guys were really friends, you must have some sense of what happened."

"They had a fight," the wife said, before she could be stopped. "One day they didn't show up to pick up the kids at soccer, and it wasn't till almost midnight when her husband came back and told the guys that she'd run out on him."

"What was the fight about?" The sister leaned forward on the couch, cupping her drink as if that alone could cool her down.

"Something about trust, we think," the wife said. "We'd been having lunch the day before—his birthday, actually—and she basically implied she didn't trust him anymore. It was terribly sad."

"And you really haven't seen any of them since?"

"My husband did."

"I did, I did." It had to be admitted, as the wife had been told back when it had been presumed any loan would be documented. "He needed some money for reasons that were unclear to me and because we were friends I didn't ask. But I never lend money to friends anyway. It's a policy of mine."

She looked around the condo, taking in our wealth. "How much did he ask for?" she said.

"I don't know. I don't remember. Maybe he didn't even say."

"My husband hates parting with any of his money," the wife explained.

"And nothing since?" the sister said.

"No, I haven't spoken to him since."

"And no one has seen her," the wife said. "I mean, really no one."

"And they had a fight, and he needed money." The sister set down her drink and rose. "I can't believe it took me this long to get out here." Her hands clenched and unclenched, and she angrily swept at her hair even though it was as stiff as crust. "Do you all have any idea where the local precinct is?" She was halfway to the door already and barely turned for an answer.

"Oh sure, sure," the wife said, looking around. "I'll go with you." She didn't even wait for an invitation or consent. She laughed nervously. "I can't believe it's coming to this."

"Now look, ladies."

They both stopped and glared as if every man were a criminal or a fool.

"I mean, if you think it would be better if I came along."

"No," they both said at once. They reached the public hall and were punching the elevator button. They stood at the door waiting for it to open, demanding it to open.

"Well, okay then. I'm happy to watch the children. Please call me if there is anything I can do."

The wife gave one of these you've-done-enough looks, one of those looks that didn't exist before you were married, and the elevator door opened and they got on and stared blankly as the door shut. Back in the apartment the children were occupied by some kind of role-playing game in the back room. On the coffee table sat the sister's unfinished iced tea, the rim of the glass faintly smudged with a practically colorless lipstick. Your wife found out what you had done, and of course she had to disappear, even from her own family, because the humiliation was so great. Why did the humiliation have to be so great? Why did sex matter so much? Whether you had it or not, whom you were having it with, whether at the time you were married or not? Why did it demand all of our attention and our rage? Why was it that a revelation of this nature wasn't anything any marriage could recover from, and how was it that you couldn't grasp that in the first place, you blind stupid shit? Just because you couldn't see or didn't like that it had to be this way didn't mean you had to go act like a man who'd lost control of his own brain.

It was no surprise when the phone rang and the wife said, "Darling, the people here at the precinct would like to talk with you. They'd like to talk with all their friends, actually."

"Of course, sweetheart. I'd be down right away except I have to be watching the kids."

"I'll come home. Then you can come down. And I'll give them everyone else's numbers."

"That's great, sweetheart. It's about time we set something in motion to solve this mystery."

"You don't think . . ."

"Of course not. I have no doubt that everyone is in fine health. But if the people of the precinct need us, then we are needed. I'll be ready to go as soon as you get here."

"I feel sick to my stomach."

"I know."

She was crying into the phone in that way of hers, which was just barely sniffling, so that a stranger could never know and could never imagine that this was the fullest expression she could ever allow herself.

"We should have done something sooner."

"We could blame ourselves for the economy, too, if you wanted. And the end of world peace. But the fact is the economy will in some sense always be solid, and somewhere there is always peace. So I'm certain about all this too."

"I'll be right home."

There'd been other moments like this one would be, when one sat in a quiet room and so carefully answered questions over the loud throbbing of one's heart. The other guys, maybe not. Still, everyone knew the code, and the code was so simple that even you in your hell-bent self-absorbed melodrama had not failed to keep it. The problem was that eventually there had to be ripples. There were always ripples. The truth was we should have killed you when we had the chance, but while the other gentlemen could talk a big game, when it came to this, they didn't want to play. Besides, killing you seemed so uncivilized. There was always a price to pay for being civil. The question was, when did the cost outweigh the value?

She came in to find her husband in a pink polo shirt, a gray summer sport coat, khakis, and subtly expensive loafers with just the hint of a tassel.

"Wow, you changed," she said.

"Just like you said. There is gravity."

"Yes," she said solemnly. It was easy to imagine that under her surface there was a certain amount of glee and thrill. "Where are the kids?"

"In the back. Watching TV."

"While Daddy primps for his interview? Honestly."

"I just this second let them turn it on."

"Sure you did." She started off down the hall without so much as a good-bye or a good luck. It had gone like this many, many times before.

At the precinct were dude guy, ad guy, and the guy who was so paranoid he sometimes wore a wig. We smiled grimly at each other when we saw we had all dressed remarkably alike. The wives had come and gone. Evidently the husbands were of greater interest.

"So."

"So."

That was all there was to say. An officer came out and looked us over. "I'm glad you all could make it on such short notice," he said. "Frankly, we don't even know what we have here. Gentlemen, according to protocol I will have to take you one at a time. Shall we proceed alphabetically?"

Going last could go either way. The waiting room was beige carpeting and white walls, and there wasn't a goddamn thing that wasn't prohibited; it was a cell without being a cell. It was good to be last; the others would have caved from the sheer boredom of it. Besides, we had done nothing to contribute to this case. What had we done? We'd been friends, was all. We met for poker, sometimes drinks. We shared a certain joy of life, though you were perhaps the most joyful and least joyful person we knew. Our children played together; they were in the same youth soccer league; we took them to parks and the zoo; we carried them on our shoulders, so they could see better and wouldn't tire so easily. Their education and their upbringing were very important to us. We worked long hours and took super-expensive vacations. We paid every cent of our tax bills. We contributed to charities. We bought tickets to the policemen's ball but never had the opportunity to attend. We refrained from most controversial political discussions. We were innocent. To fill a mind with serene blankness at such a long instant was as easy as filling a glass with water.

"At last we come to you, sir. Won't you join us?"

There were two of them, of course. There were always two of them; if there were fewer than two, then you had to worry.

We sat in matching upholstered chairs. The table was plain and bare, except for an obvious tape recorder. The detectives introduced themselves, started the tape, introduced the names of the three of us to it, today's date. The walls held no ostensible mirror, but still it was easy to gather that we were not only being observed but that we were being filmed. In the military we had been taught to contain even our own perspiration. Something like that became second nature. Something like that became effortless.

"Could you state your name, occupation and address, please?"

"Could you state how long you've known the family in question, please?"

"Could you state the last time you saw each of them?"

"Have you heard from the husband since you last saw him?"

"Have you heard from anyone who has heard from him?"

Ah, the first necessary lie.

"Absolutely not."

"Do you have any reason to suspect that something criminal has happened here?"

That was the first subjective question. That was the first question on which we might differ, but the answer was clear.

"Of course not. If I had, I would have come immediately to you."

"What do you make of this whole thing?"

"I don't know. And I rarely conjecture when I don't know. That only leads to trouble."

"Would you mind if we took your picture?"

"Would I mind if you took my picture?" Never repeat the question, you idiot. Never look like you were stalling. "Of course not."

"Often, as you probably know, it is easier to place a face among several familiar faces, especially when the face at first might seem ordinary or unremarkable. Since you gentlemen spent a good deal of time together, we can contextualize this nicely."

"Certainly."

From an empty chair beside him, the detective picked up a camera. "Just look normal."

"We photographed all the wives, too," his partner said, as they took the picture.

"It's a good idea." A bead of sweat popped out under the left anterior clavicle and was willed back into its pore.

"Thank you for coming by." They both rose. "We will be in touch if we hear anything and we expect you to do the same."

We all shook hands. There was no perspiration between us. "Of course."

Outside in the late summer sunlight, it was hard not to consider the options, so close to exposure. Photographed! Questioned at the precinct! Awaiting vilification at any moment! Soon to be exiled from one's own house with the other morons who'd been unable to keep their private lives private. A new attorney, a whole new set of furniture and dishes and linens and silver and appliances and a new DSL and all new shit, everything fucking new, as if you'd been dropped from the sky behind enemy lines and asked to survive in an entirely foreign country. She'd want full custody and at least half of everything thus far, like they all did. Thank god for that mountainous country and those quiet offshore nations, which together held one-third of everything. So all she'd get was a third. And our little girl and our two little boys. But she was a good mother. Perhaps she wasn't much else, but she was that. Why would anyone begrudge a mother of three one-third? In a certain sense that money was going down their little gullets whether we were apart or together. The only thing to do was make more money, even if it would be halved or even worse. God damn it.

"Has there been any thought," wig guy breathed on the cell line, "to finding him before they do?"

"It's too late for that. And don't call me again."

All evening and into the night trying not to pace the apartment, or trying to pace the apartment the same way she did, with the appropriate agitation and not enraged, already-entrapped agitation. There'd be so much digging that by the time they were done they'd know about our root canals and our colonoscopies, if they couldn't find you and your damn family.

At work the next day the girl put through a call from ad guy.

"Why'd you turn your cell off?"

"I didn't like the news it was bringing me. Frankly I'm surprised you're calling me here."

"Relax. They already found him."

"They did?"

"Yeah. I bought a scanner because as you know I like to know. They picked him up twenty minutes ago. A hotel at the edge of the Depths. The guy must have been hurting for cash."

"Has he been arrested?"

"Detained. On suspicion. Yada yada. You know the drill."

"Actually I don't."

"Oh sell me another. Anyway we're off the hook, right?"

"That I wouldn't say. I'm going to hang up now. But let's get together with the wives and have dinner. That kind of thing."

"Do we have to? Hey, can you imagine the questions he's being asked?"

Sometimes ad guy had the subtlety of a drag queen, when he had any subtlety at all. We all hadn't seen each other's wives since the end of soccer. It had to be done. Your story was about three seconds from the internet and it was time to circle the wagons or seal up the cracks. We were all innocent men who barely knew you. Words could not describe our shock and disgust. And now we could put nothing past you. It was time to turn the cell back on and make a call to the wife and have her reestablish us in the constellation of apparently happily married families we all knew.

"Honey, I was just thinking. How about arranging a group lunch or dinner out at one of our favorite places this weekend?"

"Sure," she said. "What a nice idea," she said. "Listen." She dropped her voice a few dozen decibels. "I've got *her* sister here. She's practically hysterical. They found him and they've got a warrant for the row house and they want her to go with them, you know, to see if anything's amiss, I guess. Do you think you could go with her? She wants a man. She says most of the police are guys and they don't really listen to women and the whole thing makes her uncomfortable and besides she's sick with fear. They're going to do some chemical treatment of the entire place, you know the kind where they can see . . ."

"Blood?"

"Yes. Even if it's been washed away. And it's going to take hours. And they've already probably waited too long. I don't know. Do you think you could go with her?"

"I've got some things to finish up, but yes, I can do that."

"She wants you to pick her up here, if that's okay. She doesn't want to ride there in a police car and she doesn't want to go down there by herself. The poor thing."

"I'll be there in thirty-five minutes."

"Thank you, honey. I mean that."

"I know, sweetheart. I know."

What had you told them? What had you done? We both knew this wasn't you. You were into psychological harm. You were into indirect harm. You were into self-harm, and god knew we should have done you the ultimate harm. The problem with the cops was that if you'd admitted something akin to vice, they'd see violence. It didn't have to be that way, but for them it was.

In the car on the way down she kept wiping her eyes of microscopic tears.

"I really appreciate this," she said.

"Please don't mention it."

Her sunglasses were jammed tight to her face as if she were skiing downhill.

"I haven't even called my father," she said.

"You know, nothing has even come to pass yet. And the fact that he turned up is likely a good sign. Do you have any idea what he's already told the police?"

"No idea." She brushed at her eye again. "God, it really is a beautiful city, isn't it?"

"It is."

"It smells like sex," she said. She gasped a laugh. "Or it looks like sex. Or if a city could look like all it wanted to do was have sex, it would look like this."

We were on the overview, heading down from the Heights, and in the distance were the opalescent water and the cypress trees and the glass and steel towers and the extravagant new hotel built in the shape of a pyramid, and all along the sidewalks were people dressed as tastefully as possible in as little as possible, slinking along, hoping to notice somebody or to have somebody notice them. Your place was off to the right, in the skein of revived pedestrian streets that was the artists' quarter.

"You've been here before?"

"To their place? Never. She said it was too small, and so I had yet to make the trip. I didn't want to spend the money on a hotel."

"Too bad. You could have stayed with us. Where are you staying now?"

"The Royal. My father insisted. He's arrived at the conclusion that it's an unsafe town."

"It can be, it can be. But I don't think it's any less safe than any other town of its size. It's too pleasant. The government understands the whole security-prosperity symbiotic thing. I read somewhere that we have more police per inhabitant than any other city in the free world. But it's not repressive. It's more like they're part of the scenery. The biggest crime here is pickpocketing or purse-snatching."

"Oh, really? I thought it would be prostitution."

"Prosti—"

"Wait. I stand corrected. It's not literally illegal, only if it's on the street. I could *never* live in a city where prostitution isn't illegal," she said bitterly. "That's sick. Do you have any idea how sick that is?"

"I confess and apologize that it is not a matter I have given a lot of thought to."

"Oh come on. They're all over the place. They're up and down that main boulevard—CityWalk, whatever it is called— and they're all around my hotel—"

"Those are tourist places."

"Okay, whatever. So it's part of the tourist industry. It's just like—" And she named the southern city that we'd all gone to together. "He went there, for god's sake. All you guys went there together. I thought that was pretty rich."

"The wives chose the city."

We were in a garage now. The car was parked. It was time to get out of the car.

"Oh please," she said. "My sister." She was tearful now. "My sister said he was never the same after he got involved with all of you guys. She knew something. I don't doubt she knew something. And I don't doubt that all of you guys might be involved in whatever happened to her." She angrily wiped at her face. It was becoming clear what we were still doing sitting in the car.

"Look, I understand how stressful everything is right now, but you cannot possibly believe half of what you just said. Otherwise what would you be doing alone in a car in a dark garage with me right now?"

"Oh, I do believe it. I do," she said. "I just wanted you to know that I am going into this with my eyes wide open. And I'm not afraid." She got out of the car and shut the door soundly.

Silently we walked down the ramp and out into the light and the heat. She walked briskly, a few paces ahead.

"I thought you said you've never been here?"

"I can read a map," she said without turning.

It was hard to blame her. She was missing a sister. It was important not to take her personally. It was important to retain absolute composure. That was something you'd not been able to do, but there were those of us who had been so tested, and who in our minds felt our behavior was justified, and who had achieved both a sense of vindication and true compartmentalization, and for us composure was rarely a problem. Or you could look at it another way and say that either sex mattered so much that monogamy couldn't possibly be an answer, or sex didn't matter at all and then who the hell cared about monogamy?

She cut through the gaggle of cops at the door of your row house as if she'd been cutting through men all her life.

"He's with me," she said, with a backward nod.

In your row house were seven or eight of them, waiting for the next step, the interior so deflated by the absence of the real people who had lived there it was obvious it had been unoccupied for the past ten weeks, all the belongings carefully separated from one another on the countertops like projects of a taxidermist.

"We haven't touched a thing," the detective who'd questioned all of us at the precinct said. "We're going to do this now, and then we're going to take the place apart, and then we're going to do it again."

"Has he said anything?" the sister asked, as she looked around at nothing in particular.

"Only that he deserves it, whatever it is. Otherwise he's told us exactly what he told the gentleman here."

"And the children?"

"He hasn't budged on them either."

"Dear lord," she said.

They closed the shutters and we were shown back onto the street while they sprayed. It really was a tight little street, and we had to stand close together and the heat pressed in from all around, the neighborhood so poorly constructed that all one could think was, you know what, there's got to be some asbestos around here. It was, in the final analysis, a dreadful neighborhood, and who knew how you could have lived there.

"What again was my sister's motivation for leaving him?"

"He won't say. He says it's a private matter."

"This gentleman knows."

"I have no idea what she's talking about, detective."

"We've questioned all the friends, ma'am. Everyone's story is exactly the same."

"Look." She bit her lip as if wrestling with what might come out. "I have a hard time believing what any of them say."

"Everyone has rights," the detective said, and it was clear they'd had at least part of this discussion before. He lit a cigarette as if to end the exchange.

"An entire family has disappeared!"

"I know, ma'am, I know. We're working on it."

The door to your row house popped open. "Lieutenant?"

He crushed the cigarette out in the street and we filed back into the dark as quietly as if we were entering a museum or a church. The row house seemed larger, as if it had swollen from the treatment. When we breathed in we couldn't smell anything significantly different, and we could barely see.

"Anything?" the lieutenant said impatiently.

"Upstairs, on the lower left corner of the bathroom mirror. And the couch up there too, on the right arm."

"Pictures?"

"Already taken."

"DNA?"

"As soon as you're done looking."

"All right, then."

We followed the lieutenant upstairs to the couch. It was an odd-shaped stain; it vaguely looked like our city. In the bathroom mirror was a splattering of small islands, an archipelago.

"God damn him," the sister said.

"Lights," the lieutenant said.

We stood around blinking at each other, our expressions adjusting to being seen.

"Do you have anything to say, sir?" the lieutenant asked.

"No, lieutenant. I have no idea what's going on here."

"I've met him," the lieutenant said with a level gaze. "I know he couldn't do a whole family by himself."

"I agree," the sister said. "But there are a number of men whom he obviously knows quite well. Maybe they—"

"We'll see," the lieutenant said. "In the meantime . . ."

"I understand, lieutenant." It was important to spare him any direct instruction. "I understand."

We went down into the tobacco-smelling street together, as mute as an old married couple.

"I can't believe he lit a cigarette," she said sadly as we headed toward the garage.

"Can I drop you anywhere?"

"The Royal, please," she answered, sounding surprisingly polite.

It was only four blocks away and she could just as easily have walked. Maybe she was afraid of the pickpockets. Maybe she wanted to study the ice in someone's veins. Maybe she wanted to tempt with an opportunity to throttle her, and then, just as one's hands were around her throat, justice would descend. We sat at a light in standstill summer traffic with the car's air conditioning blasting at our faces. We both knew we had nothing to say to each other.

"Just a few blocks more."

"I know," she said. "I just couldn't handle the heat any longer."

It was true it was a fabulously hot day. There were supposed to be about a dozen of them in every summer, so hot that you wondered why people didn't just walk around naked with spray bottles to douse themselves. It was hard to believe it was only our third summer here, but when you led these multiple lives you were doubling and tripling your time anywhere. Perhaps that was why having a secret life was so attractive to so many people. Widening your life like this was the closest anyone was going to get to immortality, and the risk was if you got caught or surrendered you narrowed to less than a life, you got as close to no life at all as you could get and still be alive. That was when the realization blasted right through the windshield.

"I bet it's his own blood."

"What?" she said.

"The blood at the apartment. I bet it's his. I bet he tried to kill himself and couldn't do it."

She looked out her window and didn't say anything. The traffic light turned and still we didn't move.

"Please tell me you're not asking me to feel sorry for him."

"Given your take on the situation, that would be absurd."

"What is it that makes you guys do such awful things?"

"His wife had left him. He was alone in the world. He couldn't face it."

"That's not what I meant."

"Then I have no idea what you meant."

"Oh, I think you do."

If there was anything to learn from a few years of a first marriage, a carefully orchestrated divorce, and enough years of a second marriage, it was to never engage, not ever. It wasn't possible to win; it was only possible to give away more of yourself. Give her nothing, and she'd have nothing.

"Did you want me to recommend some restaurants in the area of the Royal, or are you all taken care of?"

"I am taken care of, thank you," she said.

"I could say I can't believe this traffic, but I'm afraid it's typical for tourist season."

"I bet you're wondering how it is I see things so clearly."

"Not at all."

"Well let me just tell you, if it's not your husband, you don't have all that hope and trust and love to blind you. And if you've already been married once, then the speed of the clarity will spin your head."

"I see."

"There is very little that I don't instantly see."

"Are you and your sister close?"

"People don't always like the truth."

"People manage the truth."

"What's that supposed to mean?"

"The truth is like a retirement account. Some days people are all over it, they want to know every little thing about it, and some days they have no time for it whatsoever."

"Another knowing statement from a very knowing guy."

"And those numbers, you look at them, and sometimes the exact same unchanged numbers tell you one story, and sometimes they tell you another. You can't be in your retirement account every day, or it will drive you nuts."

"I'd say you were very Zen if you weren't so—" She stopped herself and opened the door. "I changed my mind. I *will* walk." She still did not slam it. There was something about her that was so alluring, that made you want to keep looking at her; it wasn't only that she was blonde. Maybe it was that she was both direct and yet so clearly conscious of not wanting to be too demonstrative, and it kept you watching to glimpse the fineness of the cracks that did emerge.

And the wife had thought this would take hours and hours.

In the lining of the sport coat was the emergency Cialis with its telltale markings shaved off. You'd need a lab to figure out what it was. It looked like a fragment of Excedrin or maybe an allergy pill or a diet pill. It wouldn't be right to say that these erector pills changed anyone's relationship to sex, but it would be right to say that if you took one then you had to be certain, because you sure as hell didn't want to be walking around otherwise. No doubt it was strange to think that fiends like us had to take something like this, but we

wanted what we wanted, and sometimes our bodies had to be
dragged along as if they belonged to somebody else entirely.
It was just like how we all had a fascination for the oldest girl
at Girls, who had to be in her forties and probably had kids,
who smoldered with experience and an almost toxic polish
that made us understand that she knew more about sex than
anyone in there and she could probably deliver a moment or
a move unfamiliar to all of us, and yet none of us had had
her. We'd thought about it, oh god we'd thought about it.
It wasn't a profession that was kind to anyone who dared to
age, and we wanted to be kind. And we didn't tend to shy
from a challenge or a danger, but for some reason, whenever
she deigned to pause before us and offer an upturned hand
that promised superior magic, we never could do it, even if
we were drawn to her. She looked nothing like any of our
wives; she looked like an older, more taut Wonder Woman,
constructed first as a cartoon super figure and then with
exercise and make-up transformed into a force of nature.
Everyone acknowledged she was the star, and we'd seen other
guys head into the back with her, but none of us dared. Why
was that? Was it because we were intimidated? Was it because
none of us wanted to spend that kind of cash on a girl in her
forties? We were businessmen but we were also on occasion
willfully blind. So why not ever her? Maybe it was because
while she oozed experience and knowledge, she didn't seem
to ooze desire. There was something about her that said that
you'd get in there and it'd be like doing an ice machine.

At the Pink Pearl they were an hour from change of shift
and the atmosphere was buoyant and expectant. The place felt
like a beauty salon or health club locker room, windowless,
clean, and filled with hair-care products. The Latvian with the
lazy husband was the clear choice and in the room there was

a drink and Greek and then a massage that she did not stop as the half hour elapsed. "This is on me," she said. "You're the last of my day, so why not?"

"I am grateful."

"You're always nice," she said. "And I can tell you exercise."

"It makes me happy that you notice."

"We notice everything. We just don't express it all the time."

After the massage, we lay there cuddling, perhaps both of us drifting in and out of sleep, perhaps neither of us.

"Okay, honey, it's time."

Outside the sun was finally going down and the pavement was sticky and soft with summer. When the cell phone came on it offered too many text messages, all speculation and rumor. When it got down to it, all of us were hens, even as we trembled over the thought of being pecked at ourselves. Was there a person in the world who hadn't wallowed in gossip and innuendo, who hadn't traded in the alluring commodity of someone else's shattered life? And then there was the problem of trying to wash one's hands of it when whatever came out of the spigot only made those hands more unimaginably soiled. Is he still in the slammer? ad guy wanted to know now. There was no point getting into that.

As she served the children dinner, the wife was jittery in an unfamiliar way. "Blood," she kept muttering, shaking her head. She'd always known that she'd known someone who had killed, that she'd married a killer, but it was you who now truly unsettled her. You were our chosen friend, you'd had holiday dinners with us, you were on the very short guest list for our villa in the south. Your youngest was sweet and your wife was sweeter. We'd let you into our life and in ways she sensed but did not say, you had violated it. "I tried calling her sister several times but there was no answer. I left messages on the cell and at the Royal, and you know how fierce the Royal is about delivering messages."

"Maybe she's shutting us out. Maybe she's had enough of all of us."

"I doubt that."

It was hard not to look at her without pity and dismissal. She couldn't see anything at all. She couldn't see what was right in front of her. She could habitually withhold what was a husband's right but then she couldn't put two and two together or she didn't want to. Sometimes there wasn't much sexy in a woman who couldn't see.

"Anyway, she's a whole lot tougher than you think."

"Of course she is," she said, scooting the children off to their evening television. "She's a retired internet journalist, for god's sake."

"A journalist?" Could this crap get any deeper? "Why'd she retire?"

The wife turned. "She got enough in the divorce settlement. Not to live well but to live enough. That's what she said. To live enough. Have you ever heard a phrase like that?"

"Sure."

"Oh, please."

"No, really. I think it's a slogan or something."

"Good lord. Could you just stop?"

"I'm serious. It's maybe attached to a vodka or a cure for baldness. Very Eastern European." The table was cleared, the dishes were done. There were still twenty-three minutes left in the kids' television show, and there didn't seem to be anything to do with our hands and our minds were racing like rodents loosed in a labyrinth baited with cheese. "So what else did her sister say?"

"She said she didn't expect the end of this to be pretty."

We both looked out our big picture window all the way to the sea, as still as a picture of stillness rather than stillness itself, the sun making everything pink as it waned near us and yet out of sight somewhere beyond the Heights.

"She can be a grim individual. She isn't at all like her sister."

"Her sister was—" We looked sharply at each other, but at least *she* had said it. "Her sister *is* a person of unique kindness and grace. I've never seen anyone so equally generous with all her children and so continuously cheerful. I mean, she didn't marry well or anything, but she never complained and you'd think she was happy."

"As happy as us?"

"She loves her children. She wants to trust her husband. So before you consider creature comforts, yes, as happy as us."

There was nothing to do with that except smile warmly. The cell stirred and it was business. "Sorry, I have to take this."

"Not to worry." She smiled and pursed her lips for a prim kiss. "I'll put the children to bed and I'll even do all the reading. You've had a long day."

"I have, I have."

There were things she did control. She controlled our sex and she controlled the tempo and the tenor of the household and except for the unrecorded expenditures she controlled the household budget. She arranged all the vacations and kept the social calendar. She had a lot of clout, and no doubt she thought she wielded most of it, except for the issue of income, but who cared about income when it was always going out the door anyway, and when there was already plenty of money in the bank? If you thought about it, it was hard to find a guy engaged in what we were engaged in who wasn't the chief earner in the household; those other guys just had affairs, and they'd have you believe they abstained from the girls because they liked the thrill of the chase or it just wasn't their scene, but it was hard to listen to them because they'd never tried, they'd never dared, they'd never known both sides of the coin. They might think they were superior, but the only truly superior ones were those who trussed themselves up in their morality and their integrity and were honest and loyal, and who in the hell would want to have dinner with any of them?

On Sunday we dug out the SUV and herded the children over to the park, where at Hades we met up with what was left of that seemingly long ago birthday crowd. The wives wanted a "normal" end-of-summer thing, though it was still August and there were still too many weeks until the start of school, as if they couldn't get out from under the season and its newly miserable associations quickly enough, and who could blame them? They took the children to their table and the four or five of us sat, cell phones at our plates, far out of earshot. Our first three desperate bottles of wine had just arrived when she walked up onto the deck. She was wearing white jeans and a buttoned white vest without a shirt and oversized sunglasses, and everything about her—her new tan, her suddenly whiter teeth, her willingness to overdress and underdress at the same time—said that she could handle the heat. Probably all of us had met her by then, all of us knew what she thought and what she was up to, but still our jaws briefly dropped and then smiles lit our faces as if we were glad to see her. She brusquely waved to us as she headed toward the wives.

"Any news?" ad guy called out.

She waved again and kept walking, the seriousness and dismissiveness of her smile distinct and constant.

"Bitch," he said only loud enough for us. Which was in part true, but still.

"Dude," dude guy said. "You've got to chill out. The poor woman is looking for her lost sister."

"She isn't lost," ad guy said. "She just doesn't want to be found."

"Exactly."

"Then how do you explain," wig guy murmured, "the total lack of credit card activity and that apparently the kids haven't registered anywhere for school for September?"

"Who told you that?"

"The sister did. She told my wife."

"Well, don't believe everything you hear. And even so, she could be setting up to homeschool them."

"I say captain did them all," ad guy said.

"But you just said—"

"I go back and forth."

"How much longer can he be held? I mean, without being charged."

"He's already out," ad guy said. "Which means the blood was his and he had no telltale scars that suggested hand-to-hand combat. Maybe he cut himself shaving."

"Have you heard from him?"

"Of course not. And if I did, I wouldn't answer. I can't be involved in this kind of shit."

The air beyond the restaurant was beginning to swim with waves of heat, and the wine was going down like water.

"So the blood was his. Good. That's what I thought. And so where is he now?"

"In the same flophouse in the Depths. That's what the sister told *my* wife," ad guy said. He grinned angrily. "I found this all out this morning, and I was sworn to secrecy. I think the wives are working on some plan to smoke him out. That's when we all go up in smoke, right? That fucker."

"Dude." Dude guy shook his head.

"It might be a good idea if we all never saw each other again," wig guy said.

"I say we order some food and I say we order a little more wine and I say we not give the sister too much credit."

They all looked around the table at that. Now was not the time to surrender. You were always pushing past paranoia and inertia. You, despite your seriousness, always loved to keep it light. There was that time your nose was bloodied in a one-punch bar fight. "I couldn't see," you protested, "I couldn't see." "You couldn't see the guy about to hit you with his fist?" we asked, before carting you to the men's room to clean up the mess. "Precisely," you said.

The waitress came and frowned at how quickly we had dispensed with the wine, as if somehow it was her fault. We ordered small salads and big bottles and she dashed off, apparently persuaded by our urgency.

"So what's the plan?"

"It's Sunday night. A night of rest. I suggest we meet at the usual place and get some."

"I'm out," wig guy said. He kept tugging at his hair, seemingly to remind himself that it was real. "If ever there was a time for laying low."

"I'm in," ad guy said.

"I'm in," dude guy said.

"And of course I'm in, as I proposed it."

"Let's ask the Turk."

It was never too late for a new character, though the Turk was hardly new. It was just that he closed only once a month. That was his routine and he kept to it, and only occasionally were any of us there for the closing.

"I'll call him."

We put him on the speaker phone. He was out on the family island, marking the late August weekend, getting ready to boat in alone that evening for the start of work the next day.

"Sure I'm in," he said.

You probably didn't even know he ever closed, but when the Turk closed he closed big. More than an hour and always afterward he emerged as if from a boxing match, staggering and slightly cross-eyed, hitching up his belt to make sure it was there, bumping into the bolted bar stools as if they had been flung in his path. The Turk was hilarious, the perfect ingredient for levity, and he was also somehow completely above suspicion. You could attribute it to his shock of orange hair or the playful array of expressions that crossed his baby face constantly and in no particular order, so that it seemed he was continuously surprised and you ought to be too. He was a gentle, kind, diligent man—he loved his work, which had something to do with expired food products—and all of us loved him and trusted him, despite the fact that only one or two of us had seen him close and, at that, just twice.

After we hung up, ad guy said, "I wish that place north of the city had never shut its doors. I wouldn't mind something a little different."

We all nodded, though none of us had ever been. The place was a rumor, a myth, an end-of-the-rainbow pot of gold, purportedly one hundred and fifty girls in a nondescript manse facing the sea. But it had gone out of business, and some of the girls had caught the next bus in and started immediately at Girls. Still they talked about the place as if of a lost empire, and it wasn't like the dinner clubs in the city on the other coast; it was more like here, where you walked in and claimed whatever you wanted and there was no negotiation.

"Yeah," dude guy said wistfully.

"Oh, tonight will be fine, gentlemen. We'll have fun."

"It's still the summer," ad guy said with sudden bitterness. "It will be mobbed."

It was staggering how our city seemed to embody summer itself, as if you couldn't possibly have experienced summer until you came here, even though it could be so deeply, so relentlessly, so inescapably hot. The green not thirty yards in front of us was so packed you literally could not see the grass. A line of crazed people waited for entrance into the Trampoline Bar, just to bounce on its floor and drink cocktails while catching air between sips. A cooling mist hung over our own restaurant, perpetrated by quietly hissing machines, as if the establishment were servicing overheated athletes taking a breather from some kind of exertion. Even an intermittent light breeze appeared to emit a white smoke, transformed into part of the weather rather than an antidote to it.

"Let's get there at nine thirty, then. The kids will be in bed, the wives will be exhausted and want nothing more than to sit their asses down and put their feet up, and with surgical precision and yet allowing time for some assessment afterward, we can be in and out in two hours."

"Done," dude guy said.

"I'm glad I thought of keeping you company," ad guy said. "I am once again fully persuaded."

"And so am I," wig guy reversed himself.

We pushed back our chairs and started to rise, only to realize we hadn't yet eaten, let alone been served our food. From their remote table the women looked over. Five bottles of wine could do that among four guys, and we hadn't even been there an hour. The hell with circling the wagons; we wanted to unhitch them and head for the hills. We'd been doing it for a long time now and damn it we were not going to stop.

"I cannot believe you're going out," the wife said as we readied the children for bed. "I mean of course I believe it. What else could I believe? But after all that drinking you guys did—you know we could *see* all the bottles—and it being a Sunday night, I just thought maybe you wouldn't mind taking a break, hell you might even need a rest."

"It's the guys, honey. You know how it is. This will be our last chance for a little while. Did I mention that the Turk was going to be there?"

"The Turk?" Her eyes lit and then dimmed. "Well, that's nice for you. He actually is a great guy. Some of the others . . ."

"Some of the others what? I thought you liked all the guys."

"I do," she said. "I do," she said again, as if convincing herself. "It's just that, well, we were talking at the table."

"Who was talking at the table?"

"You know who." She looked up solemnly from refluffing a pillow. "We don't think you guys are being terribly good influences on each other. You stay out late, you drink too much, you even smoke cigarettes for god's sake. And, well . . ." She looked sadly down at the children's cheery pillow, an elephant with a crown on its head. "You don't seem to be taking anything that's going on terribly seriously. And it is serious. And it is disturbing. And I guess we want to know why and how it is that you guys can be having such a good time in the middle of all of it. It makes me wonder about you, is what it does. I mean, a separation, a divorce, that's an entirely different thing. That's commonplace. That's—" She looked up, her eyes a sheen of unspilled tears. "Don't you get it?" she said.

She sat miserably on the bed, clutching the pillow to herself.

"I don't like feeling suspicious," she said. "I don't like feeling a vague terror at the back of things. This is real."

"I know, honey. I know."

"We just don't know what to do. The police let him go. A woman and three children have vanished. Disappeared. They're just gone."

"He didn't do anything!"

"How do you know?" Her stare was so direct that there was no choice but to look right at her so that all we could see was each other. "How does anyone know?" She brushed her eyes. "I need you to do something for me."

"What, honey? I'll do anything, I promise."

"I need you to do what no one else seems capable of doing. I need you to find out what happened." She stared hard. "I need you to find out what happened *definitively*. Otherwise . . ." She looked off, and in the look was the promise of a lifetime's remainder of suspicion, mistrust, abstinence, and perhaps even a divorce settlement. There wasn't any other way of interpreting that teary, bruised, determined look.

"Okay, okay. Consider it done."

"This is serious," she reiterated.

"I know. *I know*."

Down in front of our building was a cab but there was plenty of time to walk and the streets glowed like coals transmitting all the season's sun and heat. Hell was everywhere, and for a good while now there had been nothing left to believe in except the absolute truth that on some level everyone was a sinner. Wasn't that what religion was all about?

And what about you—what do you believe in, what have you found to shield yourself from judgment and punishment, what will you hold on to as you breathe your last?

There is a god.

There is no god.

Choose one.

The guys were already perched in the air conditioning of the bar, surrounded by four beauties wearing almost nothing and smiling as if they were certain they had already sealed the deal.

"Turk, so good to see you."

"And you. How have you been?"

We shook hands between a couple of bodies. "Not bad, not bad. I can't complain."

His pleasantly bushy eyebrows expressed what passed for consternation. "I understand there have been some developments."

"Ah, yes, a visitor has raised some suspicions and the captain's family has yet to surface. Not anything we can't transcend."

"Of course not." He smiled in his friendly, open fashion. "And besides, it's true that people do like getting nervous from time to time. It helps them feel alive."

"Exactly."

The bartender took the voucher and poured the usual drink, and soon we were all laughing and chatting. It was still early and empty, and we were enjoying all the attention in the usual regulated bursts. There were a few new girls out, too, which caught our attention and lightened the mood even more, despite our overall predicament. It was hard to say why it was that Girls could always cheer us up, but it could. It was like alcohol itself, it had a point at which it headed south, but this was not even ten fifteen on a Sunday night and that point was so distant as to be not even discernible.

"Hey, what the hell's going on down there?" ad guy said and pointed down the bar and down the stairs to the entrance, where our doorman was engaged in animated conversation with someone out on the sidewalk. He was waving his arms and visibly blocking the doorway. In all our previous times there it seemed his primary obligation was to let everybody in once they'd been duly examined, and we'd never seen him truly on guard. How he continued to wear that black suit on such a warm night was hard to fathom.

We peered around the latest set of girls. A face broke the plane of the entrance.

"Is that?"

"It isn't."

"It sure as hell is."

We leaned far back on the stools, shaded ourselves with any bodies so that she could not possibly see us.

"He'll never let her in."

"You think she saw us?"

"Who cares, we're only having a drink."

"Bitch."

"All right, all right. She's going."

The doorman would not let her cross the threshold. It simply wasn't done, unless she intended to work, and there was a whole different entrance and protocol for that.

"That was creepy," ad guy said.

"It was entirely expected. In fact, if she hadn't turned up, I would have been disappointed."

"You are so full of it."

"I am calm. And I accept the fact that she was here because I cannot change it."

"So you have a plan," the Turk said.

"Well, I know I have never been here before, but perhaps I was here tonight. I might have been. One stops so many places it is hard to keep track. And if it was this place it was a bar one of those famous exposed dads had referred one of us to—who and whom, I can't recall—and frankly I found the whole thing depressing, which is why I came home early."

"But—"

"Not so fast." The clock on the wall stated clearly our situation. "I have every intention of arriving home by 11:00 PM. You can do the math if you want. I'll do the rest. I regret that there won't be time for conversation afterward."

We were getting up to go off with our choices when a few people in the obvious blue jackets with yellow lettering interceded, so obvious that at first all we could think was that these were costumes and somebody was playing a joke. We stared blankly at them.

"Gentlemen," one of them said, swiftly stepping between us and the girls. "Some identification please. And the ladies, too, please."

Even though it was early, it felt far too late. We looked at each other bewildered beyond our verbal skills.

"We don't have any," ad guy told the police. "We're tourists."

"Gentlemen, please." A lady cop stuck out her hand. "Your identification."

"I swear to you," ad guy smiled at her, "that we have nothing on us."

"What's the deal, dude?" dude guy asked.

"Underage girls is the deal," the first cop said. He had a menacing beard, and without the jacket he would have been mistaken for some type of criminal.

"That we have no control of," ad guy said, "and no knowledge of, and we really must be going."

"Is there anything that we're doing that is illegal?" dude guy asked. "I mean, Christ, we're just sitting here having a couple of drinks."

"Of course you are," the lady cop said. "Can you please stand along the wall?"

We looked beseechingly at each other. All around the bar men were being waylaid by clusters of cops. We could see our lovely overweight cashier making the rounds, seeing what was what. She came directly over to us.

"Gentlemen," she said in front of the cops, "I believe you were just leaving?"

"That's exactly what we were doing," ad guy said.

She raised her eyebrows and we tightly followed her to the top of the stairs, where a cluster of five or six cops waited.

"Identification, please," a cop said.

"We don't have any," ad guy said patiently. "We're tourists."

The cop looked at the cashier.

"Busy night," she said.

He looked away, and when he did, the cashier looked at us and pointed down the stairs. We stepped down them and through the door and walked up the street, walking, walking, not daring to look over our shoulders to see if we were being followed.

"That was damn weird," ad guy said after more than a block.

"Underage chicks," dude guy said.

"I bet the bitch put them up to it," ad guy said.

"No fucking kidding."

We were trembling like cold school girls.

"There's another place up here," ad guy said.

"I don't think so. Tomorrow is a weekday, you know."

"Fine. Be a pussy."

We scattered in separate directions, deeply demoralized. The pavement seemed to be pounding all the way up into our heads. Around another corner she waited. How she'd known two of us would turn there was anyone's guess.

"I saw you," she said. She was wearing bright red lipstick and piercing prescription glasses, and she was pointing her cigarette at us like a damn pistol.

"Saw who?" wig guy said.

"All of you husbands. I saw every single one of you at that disgusting place."

"It's a bar, is all."

"It's called Girls, for god's sake. It's a call-girl bar. A god-damn brothel."

"We were having drinks."

"Tell me what happened to my sister."

"Nothing happened to your sister."

"Tell me what happened to my sister or I'll—"

"Listen." We both stepped forward. "We had *drinks*. Look at us. You think men like us need to pay for it? I've never been so insulted in my life."

"I am not blind," she said.

"No," wig guy said, "but we're not stupid either. Good night."

We left her standing there. In a few blocks we turned and glanced back, and at least she wasn't there.

"How much time do you think we have?" wig guy asked.

"Not a lot."

We shook hands.

"Later," he said.

"Much."

The condo was in the opposite direction, and it was all up-hill, and there were no cabs. That was the kind of night it was. She was a smart one, but what would it yield her? She had to be addressed. Every damn thing had to be addressed.

The next morning the only thing left was to text you. When you didn't respond there was worry followed imme-diately by the memory that you rarely if ever texted, that you didn't have the patience or the eye-hand for it and you actually found it cumbersome. The degree to which you were becoming irritating was stretching out like an asymptote.

"Hello," you answered on the fifth ring; clearly you had debated letting the call go. But then there was the fact of our friendship and the matter of the money.

"Hello! Are you well?"

"I'm okay," you said.

"You sound thirsty. Let me buy you a drink or a coffee or something."

"Are you sure? It's not out of the question that I'm being watched or followed or something. Even the phone could be—"

"You are indeed a person of interest, but thanks to you we are all people of interest. It's no big thing. Just meet me at that bar we met at your very first time and don't worry about it. Four today okay?"

"It's fine," you said, and hung up, perhaps thinking your call might be traced, which of course made no sense but this was new to you and so you ought to be forgiven.

There was work until then and work was what got done. The wife called once to reinstill the urgency of the day before, as if it needed to be, but otherwise there was only the process of cashing in the chips on one company and putting them into the germ of another. It had a certain excitement to it. Anything involving buying or selling had that.

You came into the bar looking—well, there was no other word for it—haunted. Thinner, grayer, more serious if that were possible. You kept glancing back over your shoulder even as you wended your way to the table.

"You weren't followed."

"How do you know?"

"Believe me, I know. And there's no tap on your phone either. Which of course makes sense and doesn't make sense. Maybe they just don't want to spend the money."

You sat with a grim smile. "You military guys."

"Exactly."

We looked across the table at each other in a frank silence.

"Look, if it's about the money."

"I told you it was a gift."

We both glanced around the bar. Everyone was always so damn happy here. We forced smiles to feel less out of place and bantered briefly with the waiter as he took our drink order. After he delivered the drinks there really was no choice.

"I need a favor from you that I know you can deliver."

"Okay." You leaned back in your chair, bracing for it.

"The women, they've been talking. Her sister hasn't helped. Things are on the verge of getting out of hand. So it would be nice if you could somehow produce your wife."

"I can't do that," you said. You looked dazedly into the air between us, as if you'd surrendered all focus, and that was when I knew, the very first time I knew, after all that time that I had no idea or I had been deluding myself. I knew that look. I'd seen it on other men before, on other occasions when they were so finished they had nothing left to admit because it had all been admitted for them, and I took it in the way I had been trained to take it, only hearing you, only seeing you, breaking down the sounds and the visuals and reconstructing them, and seeing it all too clearly.

"Oh man," I said.

We sat there very quietly, me trying to think of what had to happen here, instead of knowing it, because I remembered that I loved you. I did. We all loved each other in that strange, perilous, unlimited but constantly vigilant way that men who knew too much of each other loved each other.

"And the kids too?" I asked, and I could feel even my heart, that brick.

You looked at me again and your eyes were shining. This was all going so badly so fast, and yet it had already happened. It was over. Your own kids. I leaned in closer.

"Listen," I said. "You've got to get the fuck out of here. Frankly I don't even know why you hung around so long." Though of course I did. Maybe it was the sorrow and the guilt, maybe it was the surrendered place at the table of humanity, maybe it was the constant nagging realization that you were so much less than you'd ever thought you'd be. Whatever it was, sometimes lying in bed in the early morning of those now lost days, with all the innocent snoring softly around you, it could simply strike you that you didn't deserve to live as who you were. Then you got up and washed your face and got the coffee going and marveled at the fact that somehow you were still allowed to remain where you were, as you. It was the only thing that kept a guy like you or me alive, being allowed to remain who we were, being allowed to retain the part of ourselves that was not monstrous, the only selves that were worthy of life, the selves we guarded with more ferocity than we'd ever admit. Now you and I stayed very close. Now you and I understood there were no longer two selves to you, there was only the one self, and it was time to get on with it. "My friend, you have to disappear." I put my arm around you, because that was the only thing I could do, the only thing there was left for me to do. "You know I love you and that this is the only answer. You have to know that."

You nodded wordlessly.

"God damn it," I said. I shook my head angrily, because nobody wanted this. Nobody. "You have got to go. It's over for you here. Do you understand what I am saying? You are done. You can't come back. And if you come back you are even more done."

Again you nodded. You looked in my eyes and I could see you knew exactly what I was saying. This was over. You were over. It was a bit overwhelming. In my life I'd had any number of critical moments, but not many as overwhelming as this.

I took out a twenty and left it under the mustard bottle. I looked at my own untouched glass.

"I have to leave now," I said. "I am heading north, into the Heights, and you'll head south, into the Depths, and we'll never see each other again, and I promise in my heart that when I think of you it will not always be with disgust."

I gave you a one-armed hug and you briefly gripped onto the arm of my sport coat and let go.

I patted you on the shoulder. "Good-bye, my friend."

I pushed back my chair, stood, and walked at a normal pace to the door, let myself out, and with some restraint gathered speed, until I was walking very fast, as if late for an important appointment, but not so fast as to attract any special attention in a city where in my twenty-five months I could count on one hand the number of people I'd seen in an actual rush. I walked and walked and walked, and then I hailed a taxi and climbed in and shut the door and leaned back against the familiarly textured upholstery.

"To the height of the Heights," I told the driver. And he laughed, because he thought it was a joke.

In the emptiness of the condo I showered until the hot water ran out, and when I emerged the bathroom was steamed up even though it was deep summer. I'd thought that wasn't possible. On the mirror I wiped clear a place for my face, and I shaved, even though I had nowhere to be that night. I dressed in slacks and an expensive button-down, the one with the two-toned cuffs and the discreetly monogrammed breast pocket, and went down the hall to the kitchen where my wife was cracking eggs for what looked like a frittata, and it was one of those times when you looked at each defiled egg and wondered how anyone could eat such a thing.

"Hi," I said, kissing her on the proffered cheek. "What time is it?"

She looked at the watch on my wrist and the clock on the wall. "What's your problem?"

I went out to the living room, where the kids were building a human-sized fort with retro Lincoln Logs.

"Daddy!"

"Hi, Daddy!"

I kissed them all and stood at the picture window looking out through the summer haze at the water, just the faintest shade of darker haze within the blur of smog and heat, and waited for something to happen. In my experience when you walked around with that kind of sentence, something always did happen. That's just the way it was.

It was her cell phone first, which made sense, and when she came out from the kitchen with a spatula in her hand and looked at me it took everything I had, all the training and all the experience, to master the appropriate expression on my face. She saw I had no idea what might have come to pass. In a certain sense, truly I didn't.

"Can you come in here for a second?" she said.

"Sure," I said, knowing I must look bemused and slightly perplexed and also a little concerned. Maybe there was some annoyance there too as I hadn't had a drink yet and certainly I could have used a drink.

When she finished with "And his note said, *I am guilty of everything*," I covered my mouth and nose with both hands and let my eyes say it and it felt real because some of it was real.

After all, until there was confirmation one could never be sure. To her first question I held up a hand and shook my head.

"I'm sorry," I said in a garbled voice. "I just can't." I strode through the kitchen and up the hall and entered the bedroom and shut the door behind me and lay down atop the summer duvet and shut my eyes and over the loud beating of my heart—as if I had a heart in each ear—I willed myself to sleep.

All the next day I waited for my phone to ring, and when it didn't I wondered where the resistance was. There was always resistance somewhere, and it had to be anticipated in order to be overcome. There was a new assault from an old combatant or there was hostility or suspicion from an unexpected foe or there was doubt or confession from an inside player, or there was perhaps even an internal conflict within oneself, but where any of this was occurring now I could not sense, and it made me anxious. In the eerie silence of the condo, it seemed as though our family had decided to cut itself off from the rest of the world, not knowing what the next day would bring, because who knew what anyone would feel when it got to be like this, so hopeless and hollow.

That evening there was a text from ad guy, that your mother was due the next day to handle funeral arrangements, to be accompanied by your brother and your sister. None of us had ever met these people and even in mourning there was an element of curiosity. Meet to discuss? ad guy wrote. Or maybe not? I thought not.

The air is crazy here, dude guy e-mailed. Shock, anger, horror, as if whatever happened over the past ten weeks—and I still don't believe he did anything—has gotten telescoped into twenty-four hours. Not even the kids are sleeping, and I swear we haven't told them an iota of it.

Don't, I wrote back.

From wig guy not a word.

The Turk wrote, This is weird and there is much anguish.

There was no way to respond to that. Despair was what it was, it laid you out on the lowest floor, and it was very hard to raise yourself up in any fashion. There was so much emptiness, so much lost and missing. It was impossible not to think of the innocent contorted faces of your children, or the subtly pursed cheeks of your wife as she willed back any actual articulation of the depth of her horrific realization. But now. But now. Was she looking from within or without, or both? I scanned the papers for news, but there was none. My wife looked permanently distraught, her expression of unbounded unhappiness seemingly transfixed there on her usually bland but determined face. I had looked past her for so many years but this I could not stop staring at. This was what I must have looked like, too.

At the funeral the lieutenant milled with a few colleagues in a back corner, and your flag-draped coffin sat large and impressive up front, even though you'd already been cremated. It was something your mother wanted. She was dressed in a dark blue pant suit, and she hobbled as she walked up the aisle to greet us, playing the unnecessary role of hostess because she'd obviously rather do anything than sit and stare at the display. Your brother—a compelling likeness—sat with his hands pressed to his face. Your sister dabbed at her tears. My wife gripped my arm and nodded. To your sister's right sat your wife's sister.

"So?" I murmured.

She took hold of my arm fiercely. "Look again," she whispered.

It was your damn wife. It was everything I could do to keep myself from walking up there and taking her throat in my hands, even though this moment was what you must have wanted, had to have wanted. In a row next to her from the order of their descending height looked to be your three children. For a moment it was like viewing a perfect silhouette portrait of your family from the back, and then it was them again in all dimensions, and then it was a silhouette. My own father had had such a thing in his study, of himself with his brother and sister and mother and father, but from the front, and it was as if they had already died and been captured for posterity, certain to endure because you could only tell them by the filled-in black outline of their heads.

"She must have had her reasons," my wife said. "Oh she really must have had her reasons."

I summoned a moment of objectivity and turned back and caught the lieutenant's eye. He nodded precisely, like he'd been waiting all along for my look. Of course he'd known.

Of the service I heard not a word. They were dead to you, was\ how you convinced me, so that the emptiness in your eyes which indeed had been your own doing had led me completely astray. I had missed it because I too had wanted it. Everyone had wanted it. Confession didn't gain absolution, it just exacted punishment. Even from those who were equally guilty, because weren't they often the most bloodthirsty of all?

Afterward, your wife strode decisively up the aisle. Your five-year-old was grinning in a new suit. Your younger daughter, now fourteen, looked morose, but then again she often did. Your older daughter, now seventeen, was suddenly a woman not averse to showing a little cleavage, even sobbing as she was.

At the modest but wine-soaked reception, standing alone, still reeling, I was approached by the lieutenant.

"You know how it is," he said. "Confidentiality, breach of privacy. Though her sister was furious, the woman was within her rights to leave it all behind. I was hoping she'd show up to ease some of the pain." He sighed contentedly. "And she did."

"Sure," I said, watching my wife and your wife chat like old roommates at a college reunion. One look at her and you could see she wouldn't be giving anything away about herself. She was as composed as a Hallmark card.

"And all that wasted time and money." He shook his head, and there might have been the slightest smile, but I couldn't be sure, or in fact I was sure there was, but screw him. "You know how that is, too."

I waited. I waited and held my tongue. It was a surprising relief to stand there and not say a word, waiting for him to go. I looked at my nice shoes and smiled easily. I didn't need to make excuses, because so many of us were all the same, the opposite of aberrant. Of course we'd been transformed, but we were only who we thought we were, and we were not who anybody else thought we were. I waited, and his eyes peeled slowly from my neck, and the quiet scattered conversation around the room seemed to integrate and symphonize. When I was able to look around again, I saw all the guys had gone, leaving their triumphant wives.